CURSED MATE

SHADOW GUILD THE REBEL BOOK 5

LINSEY HALL

1

Grey

Lightning cracked over the castle on the hill, a stark reminder of the violence that had shrouded the building for centuries.

I tucked myself deeper under the eaves of the ramshackle shop, leaning against the wall as the rain poured from the roof. It created a shield of water, separating me from the city that I'd once called home.

A soft huff of wry laughter escaped me, lost to the howling wind. "Home" was too strong a word. I'd been here for only a decade, immediately after I'd been turned into a vampire. I'd been so enraptured by blood lust that I'd hardly had a sane thought the entire time. Certainly not any about "home."

Through the pouring rain, I could see the ancient buildings that crowded along the cobblestone street. The town of Siaora was entirely inhabited by supernaturals, but the population was down to a tenth of what it had once been. No one wanted to live in such a dark and dreary place. It was the Transylvania of sensationalized films, the myth that had created the legends.

In short, it was dark and dreary and downright *creepy*, to use a word that Carrow favored. The truth of Transylvania was brighter and lovelier, but not here, not in the city that Silviu had created.

My maker had been a miserable bastard, and I had no idea if he was still alive. I'd intentionally lost touch centuries ago, but I needed him now—which led me to this rainy night in this miserable town, waiting to learn whether he still crouched in that tower like the gargoyle I'd known him to be.

A pain sliced through my heart, a visceral reminder of my need for Carrow. I rubbed my chest, wincing. This damned Cursed Mate bond was hitting me hard. The work that I'd done with the blood sorceress Cyrenthia had barely lasted a few days. We'd tried to break the bond between Carrow and me, but it was too strong.

As a result, I felt my mortality creeping in on me. There was a heaviness to my footsteps now, and aches and pains that were otherwise foreign. And wounds...

I didn't heal as quickly or as easily.

My time was running out.

I thumped my head back against the stone wall, staring blindly out into the rain.

The worst part was...I missed her.

The mate bond would be there whether or not I cared for Carrow. Unfortunately for me, I *had* grown to care for her. I'd barely felt emotion in the five hundred years since I'd been turned, and then she'd appeared, and *bam.*

Feelings.

Disgusted with myself, I dragged a hand over my face.

The slightest change in the air made me stiffen. I lowered my hand and searched the night, my enhanced vision catching sight of a small figure approaching me through the rain. The streets were empty at this hour, save for her.

Finally.

The woman hurried forward, her small form clothed in simple black trousers and a jacket—the kind of clothing worn by people used to sneaking around in the shadows. Her dark hair was soaked to her skull, and her eyes blazed a brilliant silver as she stepped out of the rain about ten feet down from me.

"Devil." She inclined her head.

"Veronica. What did you find?"

"He's still there." She hiked a thumb over her shoulder in the direction of the castle. "Moldy and miserable as ever."

It was as I'd expected. He was far older than me, and immortality didn't sit well the longer one lived with it.

"He's still in his right mind?" I asked.

She nodded. "For the most part. Keeps himself entertained with books and some really terrible paintings. A couple of women who don't like him much."

I grimaced. Would that be my fate if I managed to break this bond with Carrow? Eternity alone, growing more and more disenchanted with the world as each year slipped by? Worse, I'd have to watch Carrow grow old and die.

The idea sent a shudder of misery through me, but I shook it away.

"Will he meet me?" I asked.

She nodded. "Tomorrow night. Although you'll have to pass the gauntlet to get there."

"Truly?" The gauntlet was a series of protections that guarded the ascent to the castle at the top of the hill. It was what had kept Silviu protected all these years, and the reason I'd hired Veronica to check on him. She had a shortcut specially provided by him, though she used it infrequently.

"He wants to make sure you still have what it takes," she said.

"Of course I do."

She shrugged. "You look different."

I could feel my lips turn down at the corners, and she stepped back, eyes flashing. "Good still, of course.

Kind of tortured poet-like, with the shadows under your eyes."

I could hear the truth in her voice but didn't care. It was the mere idea of changing after so many years—of not being in control of my body and mind—that bothered me.

"Thank you, Veronica." I reached into my pocket, withdrew a crisp set of notes, and passed them to her.

She took them and stuffed them in her pocket without looking. "Let me know if you need anything else."

I nodded, and she disappeared into the shadows, slipping back out into the rain. I turned away, thinking of Carrow.

I needed to find her.

Carrow

Dreams flashed through my mind, hazy and unclear. Grey, of course, always at the periphery of my thoughts. And Beatrix, my friend. She'd died over a year ago, murdered by the man who'd worked for the necromancer. That mystery had drawn me into Guild City, and in a terrible way, I supposed I had her to thank for it.

Poor Beatrix.

A tapping sound dragged me from sleep, and I rolled over, my body weighing a million pounds. Sunlight streamed through the small window set into the white plaster wall. Bright and brilliant, it slanted across the sheets, nearly blinding me when it passed over my eyes.

I blinked, the dark rafters in the sloping ceiling helping me focus my vision.

The tapping sounded again.

I turned toward the window, squinting against the light. A dark shape was silhouetted against the sun—a bird.

As I blinked and climbed out of bed, the bird coming into focus.

Eve's raven.

"What are you doing here?" I asked.

The bird didn't speak—not to me, at least—but it tilted its head like it understood.

I walked toward the window and forced the rickety thing open. The bird hopped to the side of the sill but didn't take flight. I looked past it, down onto the street.

"Eve?" I called.

My Fae friend was nowhere to be seen. The street bustled with early morning foot traffic. Supernaturals carried steaming cups of magical coffee that billowed rainbows of steam, the color depending on the enchantment on the dark brew. Energy, charm, luck, or a bit of extra intelligence—all were yours for the taking if you ordered from the right shop.

I looked up into the sky, expecting to see her hovering on her Fae wings. All I saw were fluffy white clouds against a brilliant blue sky.

I looked back down at the raven. "Where's Eve?"

The bird just tilted its head, staring at me. Something pulled in my chest. Recognition, almost. Familiarity or connection. The dream of Beatrix flashed in my mind. She stood next to me, smiling and laughing like she used to.

Pain sliced through my chest, and my hand instinctively went to my heart. I'd done a good job of banishing the sadness from my mind, but lately, it insisted on coming back.

So strange.

The bird took flight, launching itself into the gentle wind. It whirled on the breeze, then flew off toward the Shadow Guild tower.

I watched the dark, glossy wings glint in the sun, feeling like the creature was calling to me, drawing me along.

It had never done that before.

I rubbed a hand over my face as I walked toward the bedside table and grabbed my phone, then typed a quick text to Eve:

· · ·

Saw your raven. Did you need me for something?

I set the phone back down and hopped in the shower, making quick work of getting cleaned up for the job ahead. It had only been two days since the fight at the Temple of Anat—and two days since I had seen Grey.

The Cursed Mate bond between us was as strong as ever, and I could feel it pulling on me. Like it had grown, leaving an imprint on my soul. A sensory memory of Grey.

I knew he was away, trying to find a solution to our terrible problem, and I was doing the same. My gift told me that there were answers in the Shadow Guild tower. I *knew* it. I was drawn to that place like we were two enormous magnets, and there was no fighting the pull.

More than that, there were answers there that could possibly save Grey and me. It was like my power had been building toward this moment, growing stronger and stronger. And now it told me that there were answers in the many boxes that filled the long-abandoned rooms.

I hopped out of the shower and dressed in jeans and a T-shirt, both appropriately ragged for the dirty job to come. Today was the day. I could feel it. I was going to find something. And damn it, I would use it to figure out how to save us.

Eve never responded to my text. She claimed she

couldn't see the bird, but I swore that I occasionally caught her looking at it. Especially lately.

I shoved the phone into my pocket and pulled on my boots, then headed out into the living room. Cordelia, my raccoon familiar, lay on the sofa, passed out next to an empty bag of crisps. Her little paw was still shoved into the bag, and her fluffy belly faced the ceiling. I left her sleeping and stepped out on the landing outside my apartment.

The narrow stairs disappeared down toward street level. I lived on the top floor, with Mac on the one below me. She stepped out of her flat and looked up at me, grinning. "Perfect timing."

"You coming to the tower?"

She nodded. "I don't start at the Hound until later tonight, so I thought I'd help you out this morning."

We still didn't know whether we would live in our guild tower like some of the other guilds did, but we needed it cleaned out, no matter what. And she knew I hoped to find answers there.

"Thanks."

"No problem. Cordelia still sleeping?"

"Yeah. With an entire bag of crisps next to her." I shook my head. "I swear, I have to work on her diet, or she'll have a heart attack."

Mac grinned. "I helped her with those last night, so she didn't eat the whole bag."

"Really?" I'd had no idea she'd been over.

"Yeah, we watched the old *Twilight* movie while you were asleep."

"My raccoon has a better social life than I do."

Mac laughed. "You need to work on that."

"I will, just as soon as I sort out this Cursed Mate situation with Grey." I had no idea how long we had left before the curse took over his mind entirely, forcing him to drink me to death in order to save his own life. But it felt like the time was nearing. There was a heaviness to the air that was impossible to ignore.

Mac and I reached the main street, and she turned back to lock the green door behind us. The kebab place under our flats was still closed due to the early hour, but the coffee shop down the street was open and bustling.

"I'm dying for a coffee," Mac said.

"Same."

We stopped in at the little place, joining the short queue that waited along the left wall. Ten minutes later, we each clutched a steaming coffee. Mine was enchanted with a shot of mental clarity, and I was hoping it would come in handy. Mac had requested charm, though I had no clue why she thought she needed it. After all, it was just going to be the two of us getting dirty while cleaning the tower.

"The weirdest thing happened this morning," I said.

"Yeah?"

"Eve's raven visited me, then flew off toward the guild tower, as if it was leading me there."

"That's weird."

"Yeah. Why doesn't she see it?"

Mac shrugged. "Maybe she's lying. I've wondered about that. Or maybe it's not really hers. It's only been around about a year."

"What?" I flashed a look at her. "Only a year?"

She nodded. "Showed up one day, but she never saw it. So maybe it's just attracted to her Fae energy."

"What do you mean, 'Fae energy?'"

"They're earth Magica, for the most part. Connected to the life force of the earth. Animals, plants, all of that. It's one reason why Eve is so good with potions. So maybe that's what the raven likes."

"Weird to be followed by a magical animal you can't see."

"Very."

We reached the abandoned courtyard in front of our tower. Morning sunlight gleamed on the flowers filling the ramshackle space. It looked vastly better than when we'd discovered the tower a couple weeks ago. The plants had grown, green and bright, climbing up the remains of the pedestal upon which the statue of Councilor Rasla had stood.

Mac gestured to the wild garden. "I think this is Seraphia's work, don't you?"

I nodded. Our librarian friend had some kind of power over plants, though she never mentioned it. We never asked. The topic felt off limits.

The stone statue of the bastard who'd nearly destroyed the Shadow Guild in the seventeenth century was now gone, blasted into rubble, but his shadow remained. I'd been obsessed since I'd learned of him. Why had he done such terrible things to the Shadow Guild, all but destroying it and wiping it from the city's memory?

A bird's shriek sounded from the tower, and I spotted the raven sitting on the roof.

"There's your buddy." Mac tilted her head. "Does it seem a little different?"

I shrugged. "Maybe."

The raven launched itself into the air and swooped toward me. For the longest moment, I felt like I recognized the gleam in its eye.

Weird.

I shook my head and walked toward the door. Mac came with me, and we unlocked the heavy wooden thing. Pushing it open, I revealed the newly spotless room. After all our elbow grease, it looked gorgeous. The stone walls almost sparkled, and the large hearth looked inviting.

My gaze landed on the heavy wooden chair that sat next to the hearth. Cordelia had dragged it into the front room last week, and I'd avoided it ever since.

Mac caught me looking at it. "That's the leader's chair, you know. Every guild has one."

She'd told me that before, about a week ago. Apparently, she felt the need to repeat it. Probably because I'd ignored her the first time, pretending to be distracted. I studied the beautifully carved wood. It was an impressive thing, far too good for me.

"You haven't sat in it yet," Mac said. "In fact, you've hardly mentioned being leader at all."

I swallowed hard.

That's because I don't feel ready. Or worthy.

"All we've done is clean this place," she continued, her gaze knowing.

"Spit it out, Mac." She was beating around the bush. I knew her well enough by now to be able to spot it.

"We chose you as leader because it was the obvious choice. You saved this place. And I'm not saying you're being negligent in your duties or anything, just that I've noticed you shying around that chair like it's going to bite you."

I drew in a deep breath and approached it slowly, running my fingertips over the smooth wood. "I don't even know what I am. Or the extent of my magic. How can I possibly be qualified to lead?"

"We believe in you," Mac said. "You need to believe in yourself, too."

Easier said than done.

"Anyway," she continued, "this whole magic thing is a journey. You don't need to be perfect right now."

Journeys had beginnings, and I felt like I didn't know

what mine had been. I had no idea where my magic had come from. Not my father. My mother?

She'd died shortly after my birth, so I had no memories of her.

Pain sliced through me, and I scowled. I'd long since stopped thinking of her. It brought more harm than good.

But now that I was faced with my future and so much responsibility that I didn't feel ready for, I wished I could speak to her. Ask her about my past and who I was. *What* I was. Especially with my magic, which had been more stubborn lately. I could mostly control it, but not entirely. And new powers kept popping up.

The raven swooped inside, distracting me from my thoughts. This was the most I'd ever interacted with the bird, and so I followed it, cutting through the empty front room that gleamed from our recent deep clean. The bird flew up the stone spiral staircase, and I ran after it, taking the steps two at a time, with Mac pounding behind me.

My heart raced as I stepped out into a second-floor room that we hadn't yet started on.

"Is it just me, or is this exciting?" Mac asked.

"It's not just you." Something was happening—I could feel it.

The bird flew to a dusty old box in the corner and landed on the wooden top. It turned to me, eyes glinting, then pecked at the wood.

"Well, if that's not a sign, I don't know what is," Mac said.

"Yeah." I approached the box, a strange tingle of awareness racing down my arms. As I neared, the bird hopped off.

Magic radiated from the box, buzzing and bright. A chill raced over my skin as I reached for it, the bird's keen eyes on me.

What the heck was in here?

2

———

Tension tightened the air around me as I rested my fingertips against the lid of the wooden box. It was fairly large—roughly a meter by a meter—and looked old. Really old. The layer of dust on the surface was thick, and there was no lock.

"Go on," Mac said. "I'm dying over here."

I nodded, my breath coming short. It felt like something momentous was going to happen.

Quickly, I lifted the lid. Dust billowed out, and I coughed, blinking frantically against the sting.

Finally, the plume cleared, and I looked down. Fabric filled the box, folded and dull. It had probably once been a brilliant blue velvet, but it was now faded and worn. The lace that edged the sleeves was yellowed and fragile.

I frowned. "A dress?"

Mac joined me, peering down. "There might be more."

I removed it from the box. The fabric felt heavier than it should have, with something bulky moving around in the middle of the folded pile. "I think you're right."

I set the dress back in the box, since the interior of the container was the cleanest spot in the room, then rummaged around inside the fabric. My fingertips closed around a heavy object, and awareness shot through me. My magic flared, and though I didn't get a vision like I normally might, I felt the connection as I pulled it free. The object looked like a stamp of some kind—the old-fashioned sort that was used to press a blob of wax on a letter. A seal, they were called, with an emblem carved on the business side. I raised it up and inspected it.

There was an ornate symbol, along with a single word: *Rasla.*

"Huh." I shook my head. "I knew it. We're connected somehow."

"You are?"

"Yeah. I can feel it. My magic is going off like alarm bells."

"What do you see?"

"Nothing, which is rare. Normally, I'd get a vision. And I should be, but something is blocking it. Or maybe my magic is just being stubborn. It's seemed a bit wonky lately."

"You're connected to Rasla, though?"

"Somehow. I knew my obsession wasn't random."

"True that. No one would be interested in that miserable bastard unless they had good reason."

I put the seal in my pocket and reached back into the pile of fabric. My fingertips touched the leather binding of a small book, and I drew it free. As with the seal, the book pulsed with magic. A connection zipped between me and the volume, a fizz of magic that lit up my mind.

An ornate golden clasp locked the book tight, making it impossible to open. Protective magic swirled around it. "I don't think we should try to open it without a key."

My power struggled to work, trying to read information from the object in my hand. I got a flash of an image —a woman wearing the dress in the box. She looked sad. Terrified. And there was something familiar about her.

I tried to focus on her face—did she kind of look like me?—but her image faded away. Frustration seethed through me.

Damn it.

I opened my eyes, staring down at the book. "There are answers here."

"About you and Grey?"

"About everything. My past, definitely. I can just feel it. My power is screaming. And she might have looked a bit like me, which was weird. But the book isn't showing me anything else."

Mac held her hand over the lock for a second, then hissed and yanked it back. "*Definitely* don't break the lock."

"That was my thought. Feels like a strong enchantment, huh?" I looked at the clasp, unable to find the lock hole. There were three other tiny holes, though. "Must be a really tiny key."

"Yeah." Mac leaned over the box and picked up the dress, gently shaking it out. I watched, hopeful that a key might fall from the folds, but once she'd fully withdrawn the dress and shook it out without finding anything, I leaned over to look into the bottom of the box.

It was empty.

"Damn." She met my eyes. "I can start searching the rest of the boxes."

I looked at the piles of dusty, battered crates. "I doubt it's in here, but we need to search them anyway."

"My thoughts exactly." She wiped a finger through the dust on the box. "But first, I want to get rid of this. It will kill us if we disturb all of it."

My nose itched with an oncoming sneeze, as if agreeing. "Maybe Seraphia could work on the book in the meantime. She's got to have a trick for getting into locks like this."

"Great idea. Library should open any minute."

"I'm going to take it to her. Good luck with the dusting."

"Ha. Leaving me with the fun job, I see."

I grinned at her. "You really are the best. I owe you."

"A bottle of wine, at the very least."

"And a gift certificate to that Fae spa you like, because you're going to need it once you're done with this dust."

Her brows rose. "I won't say no to that."

As I turned toward the door, I caught sight of the raven. The bird's eyes had been riveted to the book, and as it lifted them, I held its gaze. "This is what you wanted me to find, isn't it?"

It didn't so much as nod, but I was sure of the answer. Quickly, I left the tower, the book clutched tight to my chest. It was small, like a diary, and I wondered if that's what it was. There was no title on the spine that I could see. The stone seal in my pocket sat heavily against my leg, and as I crossed the courtyard, I couldn't help but look at the pedestal upon which Rasla's statue had once stood.

We'd broken his curse on the Shadow Guild tower and driven his ghost from Guild City, but he was still haunting us. Worse, I felt a connection to the space where the statue had been.

I shook the thought away and hurried toward the library. The morning rush had quieted now that everyone had got to work, and I made it to Seraphia's library in record time.

The tiny Tudor building looked quiet and closed, and when I tried the door, I found it locked once more. A quick glance at the sign showed that it technically should be open.

What was the deal? This was the second time the library had been unexpectedly closed. Our friendship felt too new for me to pry, but I was worried.

I knocked on the door, tapping my foot as I waited. A few minutes passed, so I knocked harder, banging on the door like a lunatic.

"I'm coming!" Seraphia's voice filtered through the wood, and I leaned over to look in the window.

She raced for the door, her clothes looking rumpled and worn. The skinny jeans were baggy at the knee, the way they became after wearing them too long—and her faded T-shirt hung off her shoulder, the neck stretched out. Her dark hair was a mess around her head, and shadows sat below her eyes.

I frowned. Seraphia had never looked this rough before.

She pulled open the door, her complexion paler than normal. "Hey. Sorry. I must have overslept."

"In the library?"

"I live upstairs. Kind of."

I frowned, waiting for an explanation.

None came.

She stepped back and gestured for me to enter. "Come in."

I stepped into the enormous, cathedral-like space. Though the outside of the library was tiny, it was an illusion. The interior was a palace of books, so many that my mind started to fog if I tried to conceive of a total. The enormous, domed ceiling rose high overhead, reminding me more of St. Paul's than a library.

"What brings you here so early?" Seraphia asked.

"It's almost lunch."

She grimaced. "Seriously?"

"Yeah."

She rubbed a hand over her face, the gesture weary. "Oh, boy."

"You can tell me about it, you know."

Her green eyes flashed to mine, indecision flickering within. "Thanks. But I'm fine."

I nodded. *Sure.*

But I didn't say it. Pressing was a bad idea. Seraphia started to close the door and hesitated. "Eve's raven is outside."

"Really?" I turned back, spotting the glossy black feathers in the tree across the street. I shouted, "You can come in if you want!"

The bird just stared at me, and I shrugged. "That's a no."

Seraphia shut the door and turned to me. "Come on. I need tea before I can do anything."

I followed her toward the back. She led me into a small kitchen that appeared to be stuck inside a massive bookshelf. I walked between rows of books, and suddenly I stood in a little space that looked like it was from the 1940s.

"They had to carve this spot out with magic," Seraphia said. "One of the former librarians insisted on her tea breaks."

"I don't blame her."

Seraphia walked to the old AGA cooker. The metal was painted a pale pink, matching the rest of the strange old kitchen. A kettle shaped like a very ugly cat sat on the hob, and she waved a hand over it. A second later, steam billowed from the top, and the cat yowled.

"That's handy," I said.

She grinned at me. "Another request of the former librarian. The spell isn't complicated, but it's expensive. Milk and sugar?"

"Just milk, thanks."

She prepared the tea and handed me a cup. She took a sip, then sighed, her eyes suddenly looking brighter. "Now, what can I help you with?"

I handed her the book. "That lock."

She frowned at it, lips pursed. "It's a strong one. If we try to break it, I think the pages will incinerate. Do you know who owned it?"

"No. A woman, I think. Maybe from the time of Rasla."

"That old bastard?"

"The very same. We found it in the Shadow Guild tower. Mac is looking for the key, but we're not hopeful."

"Yeah, she'd have hidden it well." Seraphia flipped the book over, inspecting the back. "And I don't think it will be a normal key. But I can work on this. Might take me a little while, but I'll see what I can do."

"Thanks." I hesitated. "Not to rush you, but...I'm pretty sure that book has answers about Grey and me."

Her eyebrows shot up. "Really?"

"I don't know how, and I don't know what. But my power is telling me there's information in there."

"You're never wrong, so I'll get to work on it." Her head tilted, and her eyes brightened. "Someone is here." She strode around me and exited the kitchen.

I followed, clutching my tea. When I spotted Grey standing near the door, I nearly dropped the cup.

A shaft of sunlight streamed over his face, highlighting the curves and angles that made him look like Lucifer himself. The shadows under his eyes only accentuated his otherworldly beauty, and though he hadn't started losing weight like he had before, there was something sharper about him.

His gaze moved to me, something indecipherable flickering in the depths.

My soul felt like it fluttered inside my chest, reaching

out for him. I sucked in a quiet breath and resisted pressing a hand to my chest to force it back in.

"Grey."

"Carrow."

"I don't suppose you're here to check out a book?" Seraphia asked.

"No, I'm here for Carrow."

I'm here for Carrow. I liked the sound of that, even though everything had gone to hell.

Seraphia looked between the two of us, then gestured off to the right. "There's a small room, if you want privacy."

"Thanks." I smiled at her, then headed that way. I had no idea why he was here, but privacy sounded like the way to go.

Grey followed me, and I could feel his stare on my back. It warmed me through, and I wanted to turn and throw my arms around him. I knew it was crazy, given everything, but I still wanted it.

The little room that waited for us was a sitting room, complete with two cozy armchairs and a fireplace that flickered with flame. Bookshelves covered every wall, and about six Persian rugs overlapped each other on the floor. The scent of paper and leather binding filled the air, along with fresh flowers. I spotted the cheerful bouquet of peonies on the windowsill, then turned.

Grey waited just inside the door, his gaze on me.

Indecision tugged at me for a split second, and then

I threw my arms around him. His arms came up, and he gripped me tightly to him, seeming to melt into me in a way that should have felt heavy but instead felt blissfully light. Like being surrounded in perfect peace.

I clung to him, his scent of flickering flame and whisky wrapping around me.

"This is a bad idea," he murmured against my head.

"I don't care. I haven't seen you in two days."

"I'm sorry. I've been busy."

"Of course you have. At what?" I didn't pull away. He could explain just fine like this.

"I may have found something."

"Yeah?" This time, I pulled back to look at him, but didn't let go. "What?"

"Don't get too excited. My last plan didn't work."

"I'm hardly any further along at finding answers in the Shadow Guild tower." Unless the book panned out. "What did you find?"

"My maker is still alive, apparently. He's the oldest turned vampire, though I haven't seen him for centuries."

"He can help?"

"Possibly. If he can't, then he has connections with the most powerful seer in the vampire world. She's an expert in all matters pertaining to us. She may know a way out."

It was all we had, so it had to be enough. "Where is your maker?"

"In the town of Siaora, in Transylvania. We can leave now."

"Now? You want me to come?" I was glad but surprised. He'd been so distant and secretive lately.

He nodded. "You're half of this, and more than likely, we'll see the seer. Her gift works by touch, just like yours. If we want full answers, we both need to be there."

"It'll give Seraphia time to work on the book I found." Quickly, I filled him in.

When I finished, he nodded. "I need to stop by my flat for some things. Will you meet me there once you've collected what you need for a trip to the mountains? It could be cold."

I nodded, already thinking of how I'd stop by Eve's for some weapons. "I'll see you at yours."

Together, we left the library. On the street, we parted ways—he headed toward his tower, and I headed toward Eve's place.

I reached her shop a few minutes later, finding her buried up to her chin in books. All around her, the shelves were piled high with gleaming glass potion bottles. Every color of the rainbow glinted under the lights, making it one of the most beautiful places I'd ever seen.

Today, Eve's hair was a brilliant copper. It gleamed like freshly polished metal and was twisted into intricate braids. Her dress matched, though in a slightly darker tone.

"Hey." I shut the door quietly behind me.

She looked up, her face pale and her eyes tired. "Carrow! How are you? Figure things out with the mysterious raven?"

The bird was nowhere to be seen, and I thought she looked a bit shifty about it.

I shook my head. I was probably making that up.

"No idea what's up with the raven, but that's okay." I gestured to the books. "What's with the library here?" I was more used to her slaving over little cauldrons, not old books.

"Trying to create a new potion, but something's not working right. I was hoping I'd find answers in these." She sighed and stood. "No luck so far. How can I help you?"

"I'm going to Transylvania with Grey and was hoping you could help me out with some potions. Defensive, mostly."

"Sure thing." She came around the desk, her magic smelling like a fresh breeze and feeling like soft grass beneath my feet. "Follow me."

She led me to the back room, where she began to fill a bag with potions. As she held each bottle up and described the potion's use, I memorized it and the distinctive color and shape of its glass container. Some were for defense, some were for healing. They'd be marked, but when one was in a hurry, it was better to just grab and go.

Finished, she strode toward me and handed me the bag. "Be careful, it's dangerous there."

"What do I owe you for these?"

"A favor later."

I grinned. "Sure thing."

"Now get out of here, I have research to do." Her smile was friendly, but her eyes were tired. I debated asking again about the raven—could she seriously not see it?—but I knew the answer I'd get. And anyway, Grey was waiting.

3

———

GREY

Carrow and I arrived in Siaora three hours later. She had been delayed in meeting me at my flat, but she'd come bearing a bag of potion bombs from Eve—a wise move.

We'd used a transportation charm to make the journey. Just holding her hand as we'd walked through the portal had made my heart race.

Who the hell was I becoming?

"This is...different," she said, looking out at the darkened city. The sun hovered over the peaked roofs, and the golden glow should have made the place look beautiful. Instead, it only looked more ominous. A trick of the light made the sun look like blood on the cobblestones, and the ramshackle buildings were as dreary as ever. Though it was midday, it seemed dark as dusk. It would be worse at the castle.

"It's far different than the rest of Transylvania," I said, remembering the colorful shopfronts of my hometown in Sighișoara. And Brasov, where I'd taken her before, was also a bright, beautiful city.

But Siaora, the home of Silviu, was everything that humans thought vampires to be—dark, frightening, dreadful.

A face peeked out of a window to our right, then ducked back behind the curtain when I turned to look.

"Come," I said. "It will be an unpleasant walk up to Silviu's castle. It'd be best to make it before the weather turns."

She nodded and followed me down the street, sticking close as we passed darkened houses and stores. The streets were entirely empty, as if the citizens were afraid of stepping foot outside.

Some were, in fact.

All, actually.

With the exception of my recon trip, I hadn't been to Siaora since I'd left it hundreds of years ago. By the time I'd moved on, still deep in the throes of Silviu's blood lust, I'd terrorized the hell out of the inhabitants.

Perhaps I should make amends.

The thought startled me.

I'd never considered it before. Until now, I'd assumed that *not* killing people was the best I could do.

But maybe I owed something to these people, the descendants of those I had terrorized so long ago. They obviously still remembered me—I supposed the stories had been passed down through generations.

"What are you thinking about?" Carrow asked.

"Ah, nothing interesting." I wasn't keen to admit to my past, especially in front of the person who had inspired me to be better. I pointed to the hill that loomed over the city and the castle that sat atop it. "We're going there."

She looked up at it and swallowed hard, her neck moving. Hunger pierced me, desire following quick on its heels. My fangs lengthened in my mouth, and I pressed my lips tightly together, trying to force my teeth back to normalcy.

This was *not* appropriate.

We reached the end of town, arriving at the gravel path that led up the spine of the hill. It was the only path to the castle, a short but hellish ascent.

"You may want to zip your coat," I said.

She nodded and pulled on the zipper, drawing it up so that it closed tightly around her. We stepped onto the path, the sharp gravel shifting underfoot. It was made of a gleaming black stone that would cut like a knife if we tripped.

As we ascended, darkness fell. All around, jagged

spires of rock thrust heavenward, ominous sentinels guarding our route to the top. Soon, it was pitch black, punctuated only by cracks of lightning that lit up the sky.

"It's too early to be nighttime," Carrow said.

I nodded. "It's a curse that surrounds the castle. Or perhaps it's just Silviu's energy. I'm not sure. But it has always been this way."

She shivered. "It looks like every human movie about vampires."

"Somehow, I think this is where they found their inspiration."

We were about halfway up when the air began to chill more ferociously. Soon, it felt like the interior of a freezer or the depths of the arctic. Biting wind whipped our hair and cut into our cheeks. My eyes watered against the gale, and I squinted, tucking my head down.

The lightning struck almost continuously, and thunder boomed through the sky. As we climbed, the air seemed to seep into my bones, chilling my marrow until I felt like a sentient icicle.

Worse, it crept inside my mind. Horrible thoughts rose, the fears that haunted me at night. I could banish them while lying safe in my bed, but here, there was no fighting them. The wind pulled them out, forcing them to the front of my mind. Forcing me to walk through the gauntlet of the things that haunted me whenever I closed my eyes.

My life or hers.

The moment was coming, time marching inevitably onward. I would have to choose one day. Soon. Succumbing to the blood lust—killing Carrow—was the demon that haunted my thoughts.

It would happen without my conscious will. The beast inside me would rise, forcing me to obey. It grew stronger with each passing moment. Soon, I would take every drop of blood from her. She would be gone. Dead. Her brilliant energy would no longer grace the earth, her laughter and her kindness and her strength.

The mere thought made my insides twist horribly. It was the darkest fate I could imagine—the beast inside me taking her life. When she was gone, I would wake from the stupor, finding myself alone, guilty of the foulest crime I could imagine.

The thought nearly sent me to my knees. At the back of my consciousness, I knew that this was the magic of the gauntlet, forcing me to face my greatest fears. To wallow in them until they cut my knees out from under me.

There was only one option—one thing that might save us both.

If I were to find a way to lock myself at the bottom of the sea like I had my old nemesis, Ivan. Beneath a mountain of rock might work just as well. It would prevent the beast from rising, and eventually, the curse would take me to hell, thereby protecting Carrow.

But when did I need to attempt this? When would I no longer have control of my actions?

And could I tell her how I felt before I locked myself away?

No.

If I were to speak the words, it would be even harder to leave her. Perhaps impossible.

The idea that I might never tell her made my bones ache even more fiercely. The world had become a tunnel of darkness around me, illuminated only by strobing lightning: jagged black spears of rock piercing the sky, sharp stones underfoot, freezing cold.

Carrow leaned close to me, her shoulder pressing against mine.

The contact shocked me back to awareness, dragging me from the horrible haze that the gauntlet had cast upon my mind.

I wrapped an arm around her shoulder, pulling her close. Though her form felt cold and brittle, just like mine probably did, there was something else there.

Warmth. Connection.

A sparkling golden light seemed to flow around us, warming me from the outside. Reminding me that we were here to find an option other than death.

I clung to it, forcing one foot in front of the other. Whether Carrow dragged me or I dragged her, it was impossible to say. Maybe we dragged each other.

Minute by minute, we ascended through hell.

Finally, we reached the steps leading up to the imposing castle.

I looked upward, catching sight of the tall, midnight turrets that speared toward the clouds. Lightning crackled behind them, illuminating the structure. The stone was carved to appear sharp and serrated, the glass brilliant blood red.

The sight carried me back to the past, to the brief moment in which I'd regained consciousness after Silviu had drained me of my blood. He'd hauled my nearly dead corpse back here, dragging me over the threshold of his terrible fortress, where he would feed me his blood and force me to become like him.

I'd woken just briefly, long enough to see the castle looming overhead as he carried me inside. Then blackness. Next, I would awake a monster.

"This is better." Carrow's teeth chattered from the cold, but she was right.

It was slightly warmer, the wind no longer as bitter or as biting. The horrible memories and fears drifted away, no longer forced to the front by magic.

"That was terrible," she said. "The things I saw in my head..."

"Magic. The ascent is called the gauntlet. It's enchanted to force you to face your greatest fears."

"Well, it worked." She looked upward, her eyes widening at the sight of the castle. "This place is creepy as hell."

I nodded. "He was the worst of us."

"Was?"

"I hope he's changed. Perhaps. But the myths of vampires were based on him. He is the oldest and the most terrifying."

"No wonder your first years as a vampire were terrible, if this is where you lived."

I nodded. "Perhaps. But do not forget, I was the one responsible for my actions. No matter the influence of Silviu, I still did those things."

She nodded, dropping her head to look at the door. Not at me.

Why did I feel compelled to make her face my terrible nature?

Because it's who I am.

I shoved the thought away and pounded on the door, ready to leave the past behind and enter the future. The fact that I had to face the most horrible part of my past did not escape me, however.

A moment later, the door swung open. A slender, pale figure stared out at us. Bald, with eyes as dark as black holes, Remington looked no different than he had when I'd seen him last. He still wore the same simple dark robes that made him look like the Grim Reaper.

I nodded. "Remington."

"Devil." Remington inclined his head briefly. "The Master is expecting you."

"Not my master any longer."

Something violent flickered in Remington's eyes, but he wouldn't act on it. He stepped back and gestured for us to enter. "Come in."

I kept myself between Carrow and Remington as I entered the shadowed, barren hall. Like the exterior of the castle, the large foyer was cold and stark and miserable. The stone blocks that formed the walls were dark and sharp looking, as if one would receive a thousand cuts if a shoulder were to graze them.

As it had been in the past, only a few paltry candles lit the space, casting shadows, deep and dark. There was no doubt that monsters lurked within.

"You may wait in the salon." Remington strode across the room, and we followed.

"Someone is watching us," Carrow whispered against my ear.

The warmth of her breath made a shiver race down my spine. "More than one. The place is haunted. Keep your guard up."

She nodded, tucking closer to me.

I could feel eyes on us as we walked, but it was impossible to locate their owners. Remington showed us into a small room that I didn't recall from my past. It was bland enough—by Silviu's standards—that there was no reason I should remember it even if I had been inside.

It was roughly fifteen feet by fifteen, the wallpaper dark and the hearth flickering with a black and orange flame. A dark couch sat in front of the fire, and the room was empty save for the paintings on the wall. They were done entirely in shades of black and dark gray, the images seeming to move even though they were impossible to decipher.

"He will call on you soon." Remington inclined his head, then shut the door behind him.

"When—"

I held up a hand to cut Carrow off and made a soft *shh* noise.

She quieted, and I walked the perimeter of the room, inspecting it for any of Silviu's magical spying devices. His magic was distinct enough that I would feel it—particularly since he was my maker. It gave me a connection that others didn't have.

Near one of the paintings, a tiny black crystal was affixed to the wall. It vibrated with Silviu's magic, a sickly sweet smell of decaying flesh that had always turned my stomach.

I removed it and dropped it to the ground, then crushed it under my shoe. Once I'd determined that the room was clean, I turned to Carrow. "My apologies. I didn't want Silviu to listen in."

"He won't be mad?"

"Perhaps. Would you prefer he spy on us?"

She shrugged. "We could just not speak."

I might not have much time left with her. I didn't want to spend it in silence when I could be listening to her instead.

"It's fine," I said. "Better for him to know we are on equal footing."

"Is that the power balance here? You're equals, even though he is your maker?"

I nodded. "Once, it was not the case. When I was first turned, he possessed the power to grind me under his boot."

"I imagine that didn't work for you."

"It did not." Just the memory made my skin tighten. "In the end, it was the horrors I committed here that saved me. The depths of the depravity returned my senses to me through the blood lust. Part of me did not want to kill like that. Whatever soul I had left was resurrected in the middle of all that bloodshed. With the barest sliver of my mind returned to me, I was able to fight my way free."

"And then you were on equal footing with Silviu?"

"Yes. I was able to turn my viciousness on him. He chose me because I was strong. But he didn't realize that strength would free me from his grasp."

"So you left here."

"Yes. It took ten years, but I left."

"To go do good works?" Skepticism sounded in her voice, reminding me that she knew my reputation.

I had no intention of lying to her, however. "Hardly. I'm still not a good man, and I never have been. But I was never meant to be pure, unthinking evil."

"Like Silviu."

"Like Silviu." I shrugged. "Though perhaps he has changed."

"That's the second time you've said that. You really think so?"

"Staying the same for hundreds of years is deeply boring. Excruciatingly so. He may have changed to keep himself from going insane."

"The fact that evil insanity is our other option is not reassuring."

I chuckled, and she gave a small smile.

Standing there amidst all the darkness and horror of this place only made her shine more fiercely, golden and bright. I'd have loved her no matter what she looked like, but it felt particularly poetic that she should gleam like sunrise when placed beside the horrors of my past.

Behind us, a door creaked open, and a slice of orange light cut across the floor.

I turned and spotted Remington, who said, "The Master will see you now."

4
____

I followed Grey from the room, shying away from Remington as we walked past him. The guy gave me the creeps in the biggest way. I couldn't tell if he was a vampire or something else, but his magic made spiders crawl up my spine, and I wanted a scalding shower as soon as I got out of there.

Silviu's castle was the worst place I'd ever been, and I'd been to the Tower dungeons.

Grey stuck close to my side as we entered a long dining room. The ceiling soared overhead, skylights revealing bright white bursts of lightning. Tall windows cut through the stone walls, their edges trimmed in ornately carved black stone. The same terrible paintings watched us from the walls, the images indiscernible to my eye.

If I had to guess, I'd say they were people screaming. It didn't matter that I couldn't decipher the images. I could *feel* them.

An enormous rectangular table filled the middle of the room, laid with dozens of gold place settings and ornate candelabra dripping with black wax. At the far end of the table, a man sat.

I stutter stepped at the sight of him.

Could I really call him a man?

Not quite.

I'd once thought of Grey as the Ice Man—so cold and beautiful that he couldn't be real.

I'd been wrong.

This was the Ice Man, but he was made of something that could only be found at the farthest reaches of outer space. So cold and hard and beautiful that it hurt to look at him—and that wasn't hyperbole. It actually hurt my eyes, some kind of strange magic that was the worst I'd ever felt. He was so pale that he looked like snow, his eyes an almost translucent silver. Platinum hair flowed from his head, and it could have been beautiful if it didn't make me think of cutting my hands if I touched it.

Two beautiful women sat at either side of the table, positioned right at the corners. Compared to him, they glowed with life and vitality. Both had skin of warm gold and hair of copper. Brilliant blue eyes met mine, and I couldn't help but notice the twin pinpricks on their necks.

Fang marks.

Silviu waved his hands, and they stood, moving gracefully from the room in their sleek ballgowns.

Did they need rescuing?

Somehow, I thought not.

I was good at reading people, and there was no distress in them.

Silviu turned his gaze to us, and I barely resisted flinching under the icy stare. It hurt like hell—pain that radiated from my skin into my bones, as if he were literally shooting daggers with his eyes.

"Devil." His voice was low and deep, yet icy all the same. "It has been a long time."

"Indeed it has." Grey did not incline his head, but his voice bore no malice.

"And whom do you bring to my castle?"

"My mate." He didn't say my name, and I appreciated it.

Silviu's eyebrows rose, and something flickered in his eyes. Envy, maybe, followed by irritation. A half second later, his expression was as bland as it had been when we'd entered. He gestured to the table. "Please, sit."

Whatever meal they'd been planning to have had not yet started. Untouched silverware sat neatly by empty plates.

Grey approached, and I followed, my gaze keen on Silviu. I didn't want to look at him, but taking my eyes off him would be like looking away from a snake about to strike.

Grey took a seat that had been vacated by one of the women, indicating that I should sit next to him, farther from Silviu.

Grateful, I took the chair, trying to keep my expression bland as I looked at the vampire.

"Have a drink." Silviu flicked a hand, and a goblet of dark red liquid appeared in front of Grey.

Blood, without question.

My glass appeared as well, filled with a sparkling golden substance that was probably champagne. Still, I wasn't going to risk it.

Silviu leaned forward, staring hard at me. "Your mate? Truly?"

Grey nodded.

"How did you find her?" Silviu asked.

I didn't like being spoken about like I wasn't here. "I found him."

Silviu's gaze shot to mine. "You did, now?"

I nodded.

Silviu looked at Grey. Leaning back in his chair, he muttered, "Lucky bastard."

"I think so," Grey said.

"Though you now face death."

"I wouldn't trade knowing her for anything."

Silviu nodded as if he understood, but how could he? He didn't look like he'd ever be capable of caring for another.

"The curse does not give you long, does it?" Silviu asked.

Grey shook his head.

"Shame. All the same, I am envious. I didn't think it would happen for you. For either of us."

"You want this?" I asked, unable to help myself.

"I don't want immortality anymore," he replied. "After long enough, it becomes a curse. If I could end this life by finding my mate, I can't imagine better. Even if I only had her for a little while."

"I'm here to find a way out," Grey said. "A way around the curse."

Silviu nodded. "That is what I assumed. You want a meeting with the seer."

"I do. Can you arrange it?"

Silviu looked between the two of us, and I wondered if he would ask for a price we could not pay.

"I can try, of course," he said, his voice trailing off.

"What do you want in exchange?" Grey asked.

Silviu's eyes went to me, and a shiver went down my spine. "What are you?"

I blinked. "What am I?"

"Species. What is your magic?"

"Um—" We still didn't know exactly what I was. "I can read people and objects. A bit like a seer."

He nodded. "Can you determine whether I have a mate?"

"Maybe."

"Maybe?" His lip twisted with distaste.

"Not everything will show itself to me. But I can try." Internally, I cringed at the idea of touching him. "You couldn't ask this seer?"

"I have. Like all seers, she cannot see everything."

"Then you certainly can't expect me to."

He nodded. "You are right. But if you will try, then I will arrange a meeting with the seer."

I could suck it up and touch him for that prize. But what would he do if he didn't get the answer he wanted? Should I lie to him to get him to help us?

I hated lying about something so important.

My gaze flicked to Grey. For him, though...

This could be our only chance.

I was definitely willing to lie to the scary vampire if I had to. I could always find a way to tell him the truth later, once we'd got what we wanted.

"Do not even think of lying," Silviu said, his gaze hard.

I blinked at him again, trying to shape my features into innocent lines. "Of course not."

Damn. He'd probably be able to tell if I lied. He'd lived so long that he'd surely learned how to read people.

"Do you want me to start now?" I asked.

He inclined his head. "Yes."

I looked at Grey, who nodded.

I shifted to push my chair back, but his hand landed on my leg, gently pressing me down. He looked at Silviu. "Lay your arm on the table."

Grey didn't want me any closer to Silviu than I needed to be, and I appreciated it. I gave him a slight nod as Silviu stretched out his arm, palm down.

His dark dinner jacket was stark against his pale skin, and I raised my hand to rest my fingertips against the back of his hand. As my flesh neared his, a spark of energy passed between us.

It shocked me to my bones, a visceral lightning strike that made my eyes water. Grey gripped my thigh under that table, and I focused on his touch, grounding myself.

Slowly, I drew in a bracing breath, then rested my fingertips on the back of Silviu's hand. Another electric shock pulsed into me, and I flinched. Grey growled low in his throat, but I ignored it. Instead, I focused on Silviu, not breaking contact despite the icy cold electricity that emitted from his skin.

Do you have a mate?

I directed my magic toward that one question, hoping to find the answer he wanted. I dreaded telling him no.

At first, there was nothing. His magic seemed to create a barrier between my power and his truth.

"You need to drop your shields," I said. "I can't see past them."

He nodded, his eyes flickering with annoyance.

"It's the only way this can work," I insisted.

"Of course. Old habits die hard." Bit by bit, I felt his magical shields drop. The electricity that had pulsed through me faded, leaving behind an empty darkness.

His eyes had not lied—his soul was like a black hole in outer space, sucking in everything in its vicinity. If I wasn't careful, he'd suck me in, too. Even now, I felt hope flowing from me into him. Strength and energy.

I fought it, focusing on Grey's touch. On his presence.

Do you have a Cursed Mate?

I asked the question again, reaching out with my power, using every trick I'd learned over the last weeks.

Slowly, an image began to form in my head.

A woman, beautiful and dark. Midnight eyes that flared with life, so different than Silviu's. Full red lips and gleaming black hair. Tall and vibrant and powerful.

Her species was unknown, but she had magic. Lots of it.

My gaze flicked up to Silviu. "She's beautiful."

His eyes flared. "Who is she?"

I closed my eyes again, focusing on the image, trying to pick up anything I could find. A name, a place, a thought. Anything.

The woman stood in the middle of an enormous city,

taller than nearly everyone around her. Their faces were shielded from my view, as were the details of the buildings themselves. It was impossible to see where exactly she was, but it felt far away.

"She's in a city," I said.

"Which one?"

"I cannot see."

"Try harder." His voice cracked like a whip.

I drew in a breath and pushed with my magic, trying to see more about the woman. Nothing came. I withdrew my hand from his, immediately feeling warmer. Less miserable.

Did I want to help him find this woman?

Would she thank me for it?

I felt Grey's grip on my leg and looked at him.

The Devil of Darkvale.

He was the most feared man in Guild City. Perhaps the most feared man in Europe, save for Silviu, who never left his castle.

Most people wouldn't envy me my position at his side. They'd assume it was a prison. Yet, I didn't feel that way. Not now that I knew Grey.

Perhaps Silviu was this woman's Devil of Darkvale.

I met Silviu's cold gaze, not liking the desperation I saw in the depths. "I can work with my friend back in Guild City to turn the vision in my head into a picture for you. You can use that to find her."

A scowl slashed across his face.

"It's the best I can do," I said. "That is all my magic showed me."

He drew in a steadying breath, something cunning flashing through his eyes. The hair on the back of my neck rose, and I looked at Grey. Suspicion flickered in his gaze.

Finally, Silviu said, "Thank you. I understand this is all you can do. I will arrange for a meeting with the seer. A chamber will be made available to you while you wait."

Even though I didn't like the extra *something* in his voice, I couldn't identify it. It was the best we could do, and I would keep my guard up.

"Thank you." Grey stood.

Silviu and I joined him. Remington appeared from the shadows, and Silviu gestured to him. "Lead our guests to the Crimson Room. I will let you know when the seer will see you."

Remington led us from the room, and I couldn't help but look back at Silviu. He stared into the fire, the flickering light glinting off his pale form. It wreathed him in shades of gold that made him look almost human. Almost alive.

Then we were out the door, and Remington was leading us down a wide, dark corridor to a spiral staircase. We ascended, passing from one pool of light to the next. We reached a floor high up in the castle, then walked down another long hall.

Remington stopped outside a door. "You may wait here."

Grey entered first, and I followed, gasping at the sight of the interior.

It was magnificent.

The room filled the entire octagonal tower, each of the eight walls set with a large glass window. The sills were ornately carved stone, and the ceiling steep and peaked, covered with blooming black roses. Outside, lightning lit the sky. The red window glass made the bright flashes appear rosy and somehow soothing.

A dark pool filled the center of the space, crystal clear water revealing the gleaming black stones at the bottom. They were as round and perfect as eggs, and the water steamed delightfully.

Along one wall, an enormous bed covered half the window. Couches and tables lined the other walls, along with bookshelves and an enormous hearth.

The door shut quietly behind us, and I turned to Grey. My head felt slightly fuzzy, but I forgot that as soon as I saw him. "Have you ever been to this room?"

"No." His voice was low, sending a shiver across my skin.

I loved his voice. Somehow, however, I'd taken it for granted. But now that I was about to lose him, it made me appreciate it all the more. Deep and smooth, with a hint of gravel in opposition to his cultured accent.

His beautiful silver eyes flickered over me, filling

with heat as he took me in. Warmth rose inside me, and I traced his form, desperately wanting to touch him.

From the corner of my mind, I vaguely sensed that something was amiss. We'd just entered this room, and Grey hadn't searched it for bugs like he had the other room.

Instead, he stared at me like I was the last drink of water on earth. And I couldn't stop looking at him the same way.

I wanted him.

Bad.

I wanted to feel his lips on mine. His skin on mine. His hands.

I strode toward him, my heart thundering. My head grew fuzzier with every moment that passed.

"Carrow." Grey stepped forward, meeting me. His hands gripped my waist, pulling me to him.

5

Carrow fit perfectly into my arms. Desire surged through me as I bent to take her lips with mine.

My thoughts blurred even more as she parted her lips, her tongue darting out. I groaned and pulled her closer, careful not to clutch her too hard around the waist. She pressed her form fully against mine and wrapped her arms around my neck, tilting her head to take the kiss deeper.

All thoughts disappeared from my mind as we kissed, making it unnaturally empty.

"Come on," she whispered against my lips, pulling me toward the bed.

I growled and picked her up, wrapping her legs

around my waist as I strode around the pool and toward the bed. I stopped next to it, immensely grateful for its presence.

Silviu had put us in the perfect room.

The memory of him tugged hard at my fuzzy thoughts.

Silviu.

We were in his castle, a place to which I'd vowed never to return.

And we were about to drop our guard and have sex.

That didn't feel...right.

I pulled my lips away from Carrow's, struggling to bring my mind back to the present.

Why were we here?

Lightning struck outside, glowing rose through the tinted glass. The glow highlighted Carrow's features in a way that made her look more beautiful than ever, and it was all I could do not to fall back into her kiss.

I shook my head.

What the hell?

The thought was normal, the place was not.

I set her down, and she reached for me. "Grey. Kiss me."

"No." I gripped her shoulders and shook her gently. "Try to clear your mind."

She blinked, her gaze cloudy. "What do you mean?"

"I think we've been enchanted." I could feel it even now, seeping through my head like a mist, turning my thoughts toward Carrow. I could think of nothing but her.

It wasn't unusual for her to fill my thoughts, but even I had the control not to entirely drop my guard—and my trousers—in the middle of one of my greatest enemy's castles.

She gasped, then rubbed at her temples hard, as if trying to drive the fog away. I pinched the bridge of my nose, squeezing my eyes shut and trying to focus on our goal.

We were here to see the seer.

Silviu was finding her now.

Or was he?

I looked up at Carrow. "I'm not sure if he's actually arranging a meeting for us."

"Maybe not." She dug into the small pack she'd brought, searching for something. "I think Eve gave me a potion to help combat mental spells."

"A very useful friend to have."

"And she's fun for a night out at the pub." Carrow fumbled in the bag, shaking her head every now and again, clearly trying to keep her wits about her. She pulled out a tiny vial. "This is it."

"Is there enough?"

"I think so. Every vial is a double, she said." Carrow uncorked it and swigged back half, her eyes immediately brightening. Then they widened. "Shit." She shoved the vial at me. "Drink this."

I tossed it back, cringing slightly at the bitter taste. Within seconds, my mind had cleared. The stress and tension returned, and a moment later, the room shifted.

I blinked, taking in the new space. There were no more windows, or furniture, or deep, sparkling pools.

The room was still octagonal, but it was just stone walls and a stone floor. Not even a door.

"He tricked us," I said.

"Meant to keep us busy." She spun in a circle. "It was an impressive enchantment. Where's the exit?"

I strode to a wall, pressing my hand against the stone and trying to feel for any sort of magical signature.

There was nothing.

The stone was dead and cold beneath my palm. I walked around the room, searching for anything that might show us where the door had been hidden.

"Is there even a seer here?" Carrow asked. "Or is she long gone?"

"There should be. The seer is bound to this place, to the magic here. But I don't think Silviu is going to return and take us to a meeting."

"No, I don't think so. Is he angry at you for leaving? Is that why he's locked us up?"

"No doubt he is, but I think he's imprisoned us because he wants you to find his mate."

"Bastard. As if I'd help him now." She shook her head. "No way I'm leading that unsuspecting woman to him if he does stuff like this."

"I think that's wise." I finished my circuit of the room and turned to her. "There's no door that I can find. There must be one, but it's concealed."

She frowned. "Eve's magic should have revealed it."

"It may be hidden by another mechanism. Or it possibly disappeared entirely and was replaced with a wall."

Her face paled. "Or Silviu bricked us in while we were busy kissing."

"We'll find a way out."

She spun around, searching. "Cordelia? Can you come here?"

A moment later, the raccoon appeared in the middle of the room, looking slightly annoyed. *I was watching my stories.*

I raised my eyebrows at Carrow in query.

"She's become enamored by American soap operas," Carrow said, then looked at the raccoon. "I think you can see this is an emergency."

Cordelia spun around and looked at the room. *Well, you've gotten yourself into a pickle.*

"Yes. Can you go into the rest of the castle and sneak around? See if you can find the entrance, then return and tell us what wall it's located on?"

Cordelia nodded. *Just give me a moment.*

She disappeared. While we waited, Carrow dug around in her bag, pulling out two more glass orbs. "Looks like we've got two bombs. I don't know how powerful they are, but I don't think they'd destroy the entire room."

I walked to her and held out a hand. She passed me one of the small glass orbs. Magic vibrated against my palm, prickling and sharp. "They're powerful, but I agree. I don't think they'll collapse the roof on us."

"We just need to know which wall to throw them at."

Cordelia returned a moment later, then tilted her head, appearing to try to get her bearings. Turning, she scurried to a wall and laid a small paw on it. *This one. The door is here. I can see it from the outside but not from the inside. It's not normal—more like an outline in the stone. No wood or anything.*

"No lock?" I asked.

No.

"Weird." Carrow shrugged. "Shall we try it?"

I looked at the wall, then at Cordelia. "Could you tell how thick it is?"

No. But thick, I think.

I frowned, thinking. "If the bombs are too strong, the explosion will fill this room and kill us. But if they aren't strong enough to destroy the barrier from the inside, we'll have used them up pointlessly."

"What do you suggest?"

I looked at Cordelia. "How far can you throw a ball?"

Cordelia scoffed. *Really far.*

"Is the hallway long enough that you can stand far away from the door?"

Much longer than this room.

"Okay, good," I said. "Can you return to the hallway and throw this bomb at the door from the outside?"

Cordelia looked between Carrow and me, her gaze on the two bombs we held. *If one is good, two is better.*

"Like kebabs?" Carrow asked.

Just like kebabs.

"Okay, then," I said. "Take both. But stay far enough away to avoid the blast. And if they don't fully destroy the door, hopefully it will encourage the guards to check on us."

I can do that. Cordelia held out her little paws for the bombs, and Carrow handed them to her.

She crouched down and met the racoon's eyes. "Be careful, all right?"

Cordelia nodded. *Sure thing.*

A moment later, Cordelia disappeared.

"Come on." I gripped Carrow's hand and pulled her toward the far wall, away from the door. I moved to shield her, and she shoved at me.

"You don't have to do that," she said.

I looked down at her and just frowned. That hardly deserved a response.

"Why?" she asked.

"Because I want to protect you."

She scowled up at me. "Well, I want to protect you, too."

The corner of my mouth tugged up in a smile. "Too bad. I'm bigger."

I stood between her and the door. She tried to move aside, but a deafening explosion rocked the room.

My head rang as I glanced toward the wall where the door was meant to be. It looked normal, the stone totally undamaged.

"Damn it." My voice sounded odd inside my head.

Carrow pulled me back against the wall just as the second explosion hit. It came more loudly than the first, or so I thought. My ears were still ringing, but the blast had made my ribs vibrate.

Dust billowed toward us, and I blinked, squinting. It faded to reveal a hole in the wall right where a door might be, roughly a few meters square.

Cordelia hurtled through the opening, her eyes bright. *Guards incoming!*

I darted across the room, my hearing gradually returning. As I neared the hole in the wall, I caught sight of a large man stopping right in front of it. I reached through and grabbed the front of his shirt, yanking him through the hole.

He shouted and thrashed, and I pulled him all the way into the room, then lifted him up and snapped his neck. Bones popped, and he went limp. I threw him aside.

A second guard climbed through the hole, his hand glowing with green magic. He threw it toward me, and I dodged, barely managing to spin out of the way. It crashed into the wall, sending a painful shockwave of dark magic blasting into me.

I yanked him to me. His palm was beginning to glow again, a second blast powering up. I didn't give him a chance. Instead, I snapped his neck like I had the other and tossed him aside.

Carrow watched me with wide eyes. "That was…"

"A bit much?" Generally, I tried not to kill my opponents. Here, however, there wasn't time to fool around with grappling. We needed answers, and if Silviu found us, we'd have no chance. The guards had made their choice when they'd agreed to work for him. It was Carrow's life or theirs, and the decision was easy for me. I looked out the hole in the wall, searching the hallway beyond. It was empty. I gestured for Carrow to follow. "Come on."

I climbed out of the room and reached back for Carrow. She scrambled out behind me, and Cordelia waved from within the room. *Call me if you need me. I have a date with Luke and Laura. They're getting hitched.*

She disappeared.

I turned, then headed down the hall, Carrow at my side. We hurried through the dark halls, down staircases and past empty rooms.

Footsteps sounded from up ahead, and I pulled Carrow into a room on my right. It was empty save for a desk and a chair. Not even a single book decorated the place.

We tucked ourselves back against the door, breath held.

The footsteps grew nearer, and I tensed, ready to fight. My skin prickled with awareness, and my breath slowed, my vision sharpening in the way it did when my beast went into stalking mode.

The footsteps passed.

Carrow sagged against me. "Thank God. Let's go."

I leaned out and inspected our surroundings. "It's clear."

We sneaked out into the hall and continued our way to the very depths of the castle. Centuries had passed since I'd been there, but I still recalled every stone of the place. It had haunted my dreams for years after I'd left.

We passed two groups of guards, both of which were easy to take out. Though they had been hired to stop intruders from reaching the seer, no one *ever* broke into Silviu's castle. No one would dare.

The first group was nearly asleep at their post, propped against the wall where two hallways intersected. They faced away from us, and Carrow leaned close to whisper in my ear, "Don't kill them."

I nodded, though I still wouldn't hesitate if things became dicey. They didn't, though. I used my unnatural speed to race up behind them and knock their heads against the wall. One after the other, they slumped against the stone.

Carrow made quick work of binding the first, and I did the second. Soon, we were on our way. The next group of guards was positioned at an intersection similar to the last pair, but they were more alert. Their gazes snagged with ours as soon as we came into sight. Both were tall men with broad shoulders and dark eyes. Their magic smelled of sulfur. They raised their hands and hurled two blasts down the hallway.

I dove low, Carrow doing the same, and the magic plowed overhead. It scraped along my back, feeling like the cuts of a thousand knives. Agony flared, and my vision nearly went black. It was only through years of training that I stayed on my feet.

After the magic passed, I hurtled toward them, fear for Carrow giving me extra speed. They stumbled back, raising their hands as magic began to glow faintly around their palms. They'd need a few more seconds to charge up fully, and they wouldn't get them.

I lunged for the first, breaking his neck. As I tossed the body aside, pain flared at my shoulder, the distinctive feel of a knife plunging deep.

I spun around.

The other guard had stabbed me. He held the bloody knife in one hand and swung his other fist at my face, but I grabbed his hand and yanked him toward me, spinning him around and cranking his head to the side. His neck popped, and he went limp.

I threw him to the ground and turned to face Carrow, my heart thundering as fear chilled my skin.

She lay on the ground, her back covered in blood. Only then did I realize that my own back was sopping wet. The pain burned, and I knew the wounds wouldn't heal as quickly as they once would have. Maybe not at all.

Whatever was in the guard's magic, it really had cut us deep. Carrow had been unlucky, and the blast that had hit her had been traveling lower. It'd torn her up.

Fear turned my blood to ice as I raced to her, dropping to my knees. My presence seemed to rouse her a bit, and she groaned, trying to push herself upward.

My heart raced, fear like I'd never known filling me. "Don't move."

She hissed and lay still, her cheek pressed to the stone, her skin pale. Red blood coated the ends of her hair.

I grabbed her bag and dug around, searching for a healing draft. They all looked the same, though. I didn't understand Eve's labeling system the way Carrow did.

I raised my wrist to my mouth and bit deep, my fangs piercing the skin. Quickly, I held my wrist under her mouth, cradling her head so that her lips pressed to my skin. "Drink. It will heal you."

I hoped. My blood might be worthless by now, all

healing ability gone. But it was worth trying. "Please, Carrow. You must."

It took her a moment, but finally, she did as I commanded. She drew on my wrist, my blood flowing into her. Pleasure shot through me, so inappropriate given the circumstances but impossible not to feel.

It was like the sensation unlocked something inside me, and suddenly, I could smell her blood.

There was so *much* of it, and the beast inside me roared. Hunger gnawed at my stomach, and my fangs hurt in my mouth. My throat felt parched, and the creature inside me struggled to break free. To fall on Carrow and drink her blood.

No.

I fought it with everything I had, clenching my jaw and turning my head from her. I stopped breathing entirely, letting my lungs burn and my heart pound.

This will pass.

It had to pass.

Slowly, it faded. My head swam. I drew in a shallow breath through my mouth, desperate for air.

I resisted.

The last thing I needed was for the beast to return.

Finally, Carrow withdrew her mouth. She moaned and pushed herself upright. I turned to her, clenching my fists, knowing I couldn't touch her.

More than anything, I wanted to help her up.

But I couldn't risk it. While she was covered in

blood, the beast was too close to the surface.

"Are you all right?" I asked. "How do you feel?"

She rubbed a hand over her pale face. "Like hell." Her gaze met mine. "And I'm not sure that worked very well."

Damn it. As I'd feared.

She rose to her knees and turned. Her coat was torn, revealing wounds that gouged the skin of her back, slowly seeping blood. If they'd healed, it hadn't been by much.

"My blood is no longer as effective," I said, concern piercing me. Grief that I could not heal her. "Mortality is creeping up on me. Do you have a healing potion?"

"Yes. And at least now I'm strong enough to find it." She dug into her satchel and removed two small vials. She handed me one. "Here. For your wounds."

I took it, hating that I couldn't heal her. As I drank it down, I felt my wounds heal. I loathed that I could no longer do that on my own, loathed even more that I couldn't heal her.

Quickly, she uncorked the vial and drank.

I stood and stepped backward, my hands clenched into fists as I tried to force my fangs to recede.

"Are you all right?" she asked. "You look...off."

I nodded sharply. "Fine. But keep your distance. I... can't be trusted right now."

"You just tried to save me, though."

"I did, yes. Though I failed. And the beast inside

me…he still wants you."

She swallowed hard, her eyes going dark as she nodded. "I understand."

She pulled off her bloody, ruined jacket and moved to throw it aside.

I held out a hand. "No. We can't leave traces of our blood here. Too dangerous. We don't know how Silviu will use it."

"Good point." She shoved it into her bag.

I searched the ground where we'd fallen, looking for signs of our blood. Our clothes seemed to have soaked up most of it, thank fates. There were a few small, quickly drying specks that would be of no use to Silviu.

"Let's keep moving." I turned to head down the hall.

We walked swiftly and silently, passing the bodies of the guards without a second glance. We'd need to be quick to find the seer, but once we had, the magic in the seer's cavern would prevent us from being disturbed.

As we descended a sloped hallway, it grew colder and colder, as if the castle were built into a hill of ice. Carrow shivered. "We're close, aren't we?"

"Yes. Those were the last guards, I believe." I'd never come down here much when I'd lived in the castle, but I was fairly certain.

"It also feels like hell." She rubbed her arms.

She was right, I realized. A prickling sensation raced across my skin. This whole place was foul with dark magic.

6

———

A moment later, we reached a heavy wooden door at the end of the corridor a dozen yards past the last guards.

"To my knowledge," Grey said, "we're at ground level. This should lead us to the seer's cavern."

The magic that pulsed from the door made my insides churn. I pressed a hand to my stomach and breathed deeply. "Is this why the guards were positioned so far away?"

Grey nodded. "It's impossible to stay long in this spot. Come on."

He reached for the iron door handle and pushed inward. As the heavy door swung open, the magic became more repulsive.

I drew in an unsteady breath. "This is awful."

"We just need to get through, then it will be better." He entered the dark corridor, and I followed.

Immediately, stairs descended. We took them two at a time, hurrying into the darkness. Every three meters or so, torches on the walls burst to life as we passed. Their glow was faint but welcome.

It took us at least five minutes to descend the entire way. We had to be a dozen stories underground. The air grew icy and damp, and I rubbed my arms, wishing my jacket hadn't been ruined. The wet, blood-soaked shirt at my back turned hard, freezing in the air. My teeth chattered.

"Almost there," Grey said.

We reached a huge room at the base of the stairs, a cavern carved right out of the black rock. Icicles hung from the ceiling, and a white mist filled the otherwise empty space.

"Who could possibly live down here?" I asked.

"The seer is not actually a person," Grey said. "It's a shadow from the past. The collective memories and knowledge of all turned vampires."

"Wow." I'd had no idea that was even possible.

"Come." He reached for my hand, but right before our fingers could touch, he drew his hand back and clenched it into a fist. He shook his head. "Not safe. Follow me."

I searched his face, looking for the beast that so

terrified him. What was it like to have a monster inside you that would force you to do its will?

Terrible.

Normally, he had it under control without issue. But with this curse growing stronger by the day…

He turned and walked toward the center of the cavern. I followed, moving deeper into the mist. It flowed around me, icy cold, and I felt its touch everywhere. Almost as if it were trying to know me.

"Stop here." Grey's voice was soft.

We stopped.

The mist swirled, kicking up a breeze, then coalesced in the middle of the cavern, growing thicker and whiter right in front of us. It reached critical mass, then fell to the ground in a splash of opalescent water that lapped gently toward the tips of our boots.

Grey stepped back, and I mimicked the movement.

Breath held, I watched the water. It rose upward, forming an ethereal figure with no gender or race. The features were indistinct, but a sense of wisdom emanated from it.

Grey bowed, and I copied the gesture, not able to take my gaze from the strange form. I'd seen a lot of weird stuff during my time in the magical realm, but this might take the cake.

We straightened.

"Why have you wakened me?" the seer asked, its voice echoing with power that shook my bones.

"Thank you for appearing," Grey said. "We are here for help, if you are so inclined."

"Of what sort?"

"We are Cursed Mates," he said.

The figure tilted its head, then drifted forward, so close that I could see through it to the other side of the cavern wall. The seer reached out an indistinct hand, hovering it over my chest, then over Grey's.

"Yes, I can feel that. It has been a very long time since I have seen a pair of you. I assume you are here because you want to break the curse?"

Grey nodded. "We'd both like to survive."

"Do you want to break the bond as well?" the seer asked.

Shock raced through me.

Break the mate bond?

I'd assumed it wasn't possible. After we'd tried with Cyrenthia's magic and failed, I'd assumed it was something that would always be there.

Did I *want* to break the bond with him?

Did it matter?

Even though we'd temporarily severed it, I'd still felt so strongly for him.

"You are uncertain," the seer said. "Which is not unexpected."

I said nothing. I'd never been quite so out of my depth as I was then.

"Is it possible to break the curse?" Grey asked.

The seer raised a shoulder in a shrug. "Not that I have ever seen."

"So there is no hope?" Grey asked.

"A moment, please." The seer drifted toward me, its form moving quickly.

My heart leapt, and I moved to step back, but I was too slow. The seer's entire ethereal body flowed right into mine, freezing cold.

Suddenly, my soul felt full to bursting, like energy was blasting around inside my body, inspecting every inch of me.

I gasped and reached for Grey. He gripped my arm, helping me stand upright. My head spun and my vision went fuzzy as the energy grew and grew.

Finally, it exploded out of me. I sucked at the air, my body suddenly empty and warm.

Normal.

Panting, I looked up.

The seer stood in front of me, looking the same as ever.

"A little warning next time," I said, panting.

Grey kept me on my feet until my limbs stopped shaking. Looking at him, I asked, "Did you know that would happen?"

He shook his head.

I looked back at the seer. "What did you see?"

"Cursed Mates almost never survive. They aren't powerful enough. But you...I think you might be."

"How?"

"The answer is inside you. Inside your power. You doubt yourself and your ability to lead because you don't understand what you are. But knowing your past will help you know your power."

My ability to lead. My mind flashed to the leader's chair I'd been unable to sit in. To Mac's words. But how was I even qualified? "What power?" I barely understood my magic.

"The answers are in your past, but you must find them yourself. This is something I cannot see."

"What about my past? *Where* in my past?" Again, I wished I'd known my mother. I couldn't stop thinking of her lately, wishing that she'd survived so I could know her. Learn from her.

"That is for you to discover. Once you know what you are, what your *true* power is, you will have your answers. You will be able to save him."

"I'm a seer."

"No, you aren't."

It was right. The Seer's Guild had never claimed me. Though I had a gift similar to a seer's, I wasn't actually one of them.

"Come." The figure motioned me forward. "Let me see if there is anything inside your mind."

"Are you going to do that thing again?" I asked.

"No. Then, I was looking at your magic. At your soul. This is different."

I approached, my heart racing. The figure rested cold fingertips against my temple. They felt like an icy mist—there, but not. The chill seeped inside my head, seeming to float around inside my mind. Searching.

"Your memories…"

I looked at the seer, wanting it to continue. To speak more quickly. Finally, it did. "You have recently found a book. Your answers are there. Your friend will help you."

"Seraphia?"

"No. The raven."

"The raven?" Confusion flickered. "Eve's raven?"

"Not Eve's. Yours. The raven waits with Eve, drawn by her Fae energy. It is life, keeping the raven here while it waits."

"I don't understand."

"You will. But first, you must open the book and find your past."

"Seraphia is working on the book."

"And she will be successful," the seer said. "But it will take your blood to finish the spell that will open the book. Then you must find the raven."

"What about the raven? And I'll just read all the answers in the book?" It definitely sounded too easy, especially given how difficult and unpredictable my magic could be. My skills were improving, but erratically.

It laughed—or at least made a sound that might have been a laugh, raspy and rough. "No, nothing so simple. But it will be a guide, helping you along the path to discovering what you are and what you can do. Once you know, you will be able to save them both."

"Both? Grey and me?"

The seer disappeared, its form fading out into mist that once again filled the chamber. I looked at Grey, almost more confused than when I'd arrived.

He rubbed a hand over his face. "That was...not bad."

"Not bad? I have no idea what to do."

"No, we don't know *exactly* what to do. But we have plenty of clues now. And the seer is gone. We need to leave."

I nodded, my mind racing to catalog and memorize everything the seer had told me. Obviously, we needed to get to Seraphia immediately. And the raven...

We had to find that bird, whatever that meant.

"Can we transport?" I asked Grey, wanting to avoid the trip back through the castle.

"Not until we are outside. Silviu would never let his prey go so easily." He turned and headed toward the stairs.

I followed, racing up behind him.

The corridors were empty as we hurried toward the exit. The bodies of the guards lay still and undisturbed, and I began to hope that we would make it out of there without trouble.

We were nearly to the exit when a voice boomed behind us. "Devil."

We spun around, spotting Silviu on the other side of the room.

He stood on the stairs, his tall form stiff. His black suit was so perfectly pressed and he stood so still that he looked like a mannequin in a department store in Hell.

"Silviu." Grey's voice sounded bored. "We are leaving now."

"I need her. You know that."

"I'm afraid you cannot have her." He stepped forward.

"No," I whispered.

"I'll handle this," he said. "Get out of here."

"The point is for both of us to survive. I'm not leaving you."

"I cannot allow you to depart so soon," Silviu said.

"This isn't the way to obtain Carrow's help," Grey said. "You've been cooped up here too long. You no longer know how to engage with people."

Silviu shrugged a slim shoulder. "Perhaps you are right and I am out of date. All the same, I like things my way."

I scoffed, watching him, looking for any kind of weakness that I could exploit. I wouldn't jump on it—not unless Grey really needed me to. But this was his maker. His fight.

"Unfortunately, you cannot have things your way,"

Grey said. "I proved that last time when I left here, and I'm going to do so again."

A shadow of rage passed over Silviu's face, and he raised a hand. It burned bright red with flame, and he hurled the fireball directly at Grey.

Instead of dodging, Grey stepped into it, taking the blast on the chest. It exploded around him, enveloping his form, and he seemed to glow briefly, growing stronger.

"You've forgotten my particular talent," Grey said, a smile in his voice.

"Bastard," Silviu hissed, annoyance in the tone.

"I learned the gift here, you know." Grey approached slowly, like a predator. "Adapted to survive. To escape."

"You'll not escape this time." Silviu prowled closer.

Grey

Silviu stared at me, rage in his eyes. His time alone in this castle had twisted his mind. He was still powerful—massively so.

But rage drove him now.

He would make mistakes.

It made it even easier to manipulate his thoughts.

I imbued my voice with power, letting my magic flow

through my words and into him. "You will let us leave unharmed."

"You know that does not work on me," Silviu muttered, stalking closer, moving like a panther out for a kill.

"Doesn't work *well*." I smiled. "But it does work."

He growled.

"You will not fight us," I said.

His steps stuttered, as if his body fought to stop him from walking, yet his mind wanted to force him to keep going. He pushed onward, moving more slowly, his brow furrowed with effort.

"I will punish you for this," he hissed.

"Your ability to do that disappeared long ago." I charged, hurtling toward him with every bit of speed and rage that filled my body.

Protect.

I could feel Carrow behind me, no doubt debating which angle to attack from. I wanted to finish this before she even tried. She shouldn't be anywhere near Silviu.

I reached him a half second later, raising my fist and delivering a swift punch to his jaw. He spun backward, staggering. The pain seemed to have shocked him free of my mind control, and he whirled toward me, slamming me down.

He fell upon me, swinging for my face as his speed took me to the ground. Before he could land the blow, I kicked up, hitting him in the stomach and hurling him off of me.

He flew into the nearby wall. I stood, and he straightened. We collided in a blur of fists. Silviu landed a hard blow to my jaw, making pain flare. I felt the bone crack, the agony nearly blinding me. Instinct drove my movements, and I returned the blow, striking twice in a row.

Thoughts of Carrow fueled me, making me stronger, faster.

Silviu raised a fist for another punch, but I blocked, putting all my strength into my next blow. My fist slammed into his jaw, radiating pain up my arm. He sailed backward and landed in a heap, lying still.

Unconscious.

I turned toward Carrow, who stood nearby, a dagger and a potion bomb clutched in each hand.

"You never gave me an opening," she said.

The corner of my mouth quirked up in a small smile, but pain from my broken jaw made starbursts explode behind my eyes. "Come. He'll regain consciousness soon."

She nodded, and we hurried from the castle, racing down the steps and onto the gravel path. We sprinted downward through the gauntlet, the freezing cold piercing my bones.

We were nearly to the end when I heard a shout from above. The rage that echoed in the sound competed with the blasts of thunder that tore through the sky.

Silviu.

I looked back, spotting the tiny, pale figure of my maker standing at the door to his castle.

He'd always been a bastard.

I turned back and raced alongside Carrow. A dozen meters later, and I felt the protective charm that surrounded the castle break.

I grabbed her hand and pulled her to a stop. "We can transport from here."

"Thank fates." She spun toward me, face pale and lips shaking with cold.

I plunged my hand into my pocket and withdrew a transport charm. Quickly, I slammed it to the ground. A silvery gray cloud exploded upward, and I gripped Carrow's hand tightly, imagining the courtyard outside of my tower.

Together, we stepped into the mist. The ether sucked us in and pulled us through space, spinning us wildly until my feet landed on the cobblestones of Guild City.

Night had fallen, the sky dark and the city streets nearly empty. Streetlamps flickered with a golden glow, giving Carrow's pale face some color.

She heaved a sigh and tipped her head back. "That was close. No wonder you got the hell out of there as soon as you could."

I nodded. "It was an unpleasant decade."

My shirt stuck to my back, torn and bloody. Though those wounds had healed, I was a mess and needed another healing potion for my jaw. My natural healing was gone now. "I haven't had a hit like that in a while."

"He was powerful." Worry twisted her mouth. "Are you all right?"

"Fine."

"Will he come for us?"

"Possible, but doubtful. He hasn't left that castle in centuries. I'm not sure he knows how anymore."

"Good."

"I need a change of clothes," I said, feeling the wind on my back through my torn shirt. My jaw ached, a reminder of the mortality biting at my heels. I needed to seek another healing potion immediately. "I assume you want to return to the library?"

"I do." She shifted, pulling at her ruined shirt. "But do you mind if I get cleaned up at your place first?"

"Not at all."

7

CARROW

It didn't take long to get cleaned up and borrow a shirt from Grey. It was far too big, but I tied it at my waist and rolled up the sleeves.

The worst—best—part was that the shirt smelled like him. I drew in a deep breath, though I knew that wasn't smart. His scent filled my head, sending me back to the last time we'd kissed. Heat thrummed through my veins, and my skin prickled with awareness.

"Are you ready?"

Grey's voice dragged me from my thoughts, and I blinked at him, returning to the present.

I stood in his living room, right in front of the bookshelves. He'd just changed and stood at the door to his bedroom, looking handsome as ever in dark trousers and a sweater. His jaw was no longer slightly swollen, and his hair was damp from a shower.

"Yes. Let's go." As much as I wanted to spend the night there with Grey, the thought of the answers the book might hold got me moving.

We left the tower in silence, passing Miranda at the hostess station and the guards at the front door. When we were in the courtyard and alone, Grey spoke. "The seer mentioned your past as being important to this, but you've never spoken of it."

Somehow, I wasn't surprised to hear him mention it. He was right—I *never* spoke of it.

"That's because I hardly ever think about it," I said.

"Really?"

I nodded. "As a child, I became very good at compartmentalizing. It's a useful talent."

"I'm aware."

I looked up at him, spotting a wry grin on his face. We were passing a brightly lit shop full of potion bottles. The lights from within flickered in his eyes, which were shadowed with misery, no doubt at the memory of his past. Of course he'd be good at compartmentalizing after the life he'd led.

"I guess we have that in common," I said.

"What?"

"Pasts we don't think of."

"I can't imagine yours is full of murder and terrorizing you'd rather forget."

"It's not. But you need to remember that you weren't in control then." We passed a coffee shop, the interior bustling with people who laughed and talked. It was a such a contrast to our conversation.

"I may have been controlled by the monster within, but it was still *me* who did those things. I bear responsibility." I could feel the burn of his gaze, and I looked up to catch him staring at me. When he spoke again, his voice was soft, "What are you trying to forget?"

"Nothing as bad as your memories. Not nearly." But still, I hated to think of it. Hated to speak of it.

Somehow, though, walking on the quiet street made it easier to face. There was just enough distraction to keep me from sinking into it, and I didn't have to make eye contact, which helped.

"Tell me," he said.

"It's all very human and mundane," I said. "Just a miserable childhood that I would like to leave in the past."

"Yet, somehow, it's connected to this."

I sighed, nodding. He was right. If we wanted to get to the bottom of this mess, I'd have to revisit the past I'd done such a good job of suppressing. "My mother died shortly after I was born. Car crash." Again, the ache that I'd numbed for so long. Being forced to confront my past made me face how much I missed her.

"And your father?"

"An alcoholic. Barely knew him, even though we lived in the same house." I shuddered at the memory. He occupied the place of bogeyman in my mind, a shadowy figure whom I'd forced into the closet.

"He sounds like a miserable bastard."

"He was. Logically, I know that alcoholism is a disease, and part of me feels for him. He never got the help he needed. But then there's the rest of me...the child that lived with him. That feared him..."

He reached for my hand, gripping it tight. "I wish I could go back and save you."

The tiniest bit of warmth glowed against the cold-ness of my soul. "Thanks. But it didn't last forever. I grew up and got out. Met Beatrix. Things were better then."

My throat tightened at the memory of my friend. A bird's cry sounded from high above, and I looked up.

The raven flew overhead, following me once again. We were nearly to the library, only a few blocks away, but quite far from Eve's shop, where the raven usually spent its time.

What was it with that bird? If only the seer hadn't been so opaque.

"Were both your parents magical?" he asked.

I shrugged. "Not my father. And my mother...I don't know."

"You don't think of her?"

"Absolutely not." Just the idea of it made my heart

hurt. "There was a time when I wondered about her. I was still little enough to have fantasies that she would come and get me. But those got me nowhere. Eventually, I grew old enough to realize they were ridiculous and hurting me. So I stopped thinking of her." My technique had worked for the longest time, too.

No longer.

"That takes a powerful will."

"One thing I've got. I don't know when to quit—even when it would be smart." My drive had kept me doggedly going after criminals in the human world. Had gotten me arrested for a murder I didn't commit. "So my mother must have been a supernatural?"

"Yes, more than likely. Magical talent is most often genetic. Given what the seer said, I think that's the case for you."

I nodded. How such an ancient book was going to tell me about my past, I had no idea. But it was our only lead.

We arrived at the library a moment later. Golden light shone from the small windows on either side of the door, which was unlocked. I slipped inside, Grey close at my heels.

"Back here," Seraphia shouted.

I followed her voice toward the rear of the library, where she'd set up a workstation at a large wooden table. It was covered with books and various small tools

—knives and brushes and little pots that glowed with light.

She looked up from her seat at the table, her dark hair messy and her eyes shadowed. She still wore the ratty T-shirt and jeans, and she looked like a far different woman than the one I'd first met outside my shop.

Something was up with Seraphia.

I hurried to her side. "Have you been working on this all day?"

"Yes."

"You look exhausted." I stared at the book, hoping it hadn't been completely devouring her time and energy.

"It's not the book's fault. I've got some...things going on." She shook her head. "But don't worry about that. Look here." She pointed to the book, which lay on the table underneath a small lamp, then maneuvered a large magnifying glass over the golden clasp.

Grey crowded close, and we both peered at the book. Beneath the magnifying glass, it was possible to see tiny grooves carved into the metal. She pointed to them. "This is the lock. There's no key for it, but I think you're meant to put a liquid in there. It would travel through the grooves, into the interior, then open it. But I have no idea what type of liquid, and if we get it wrong, the journal will probably self-destruct."

"It's my blood," I said, remembering what the seer had told me.

Seraphia's gaze flicked to me, eyebrows raised.

"Blood makes sense. How do you know it's meant to be yours?"

"A seer told us. It's something to do with my past."

"An ancestor of yours might have written this book, then?"

"Maybe."

"Okay, then." She pointed to the book, indicating the three small holes drilled into the metal clasp. "I think two of these holes are meant to trick you. Ignore them. Place a small drop of blood in this hole near the edge. That's the proper starting point."

I drew in an unsteady breath, wondering what we were going to find. It'd been so long since I'd thought of my past, and now I'd been handed a gift.

"Here." Seraphia handed me a small dagger. "It's clean."

I took it, then raised it to my finger and pricked. The blood welled, and I dripped a tiny droplet into the hole in the golden clasp. Through the magnifying glass, we watched the blood race along the intricately curved channels. It shot through quickly, and magic began to glow around the book, brighter and brighter, until the clasp was so brilliant, I had to squint. With a pop, the clasp broke open, and the front cover lifted slightly.

"Perfect!" Seraphia picked up the book and handed it to me. "You should maybe read it on your own, if it's about you."

"Thanks." I took the book, feeling the faintest pulse of magic.

She shooed me toward the door. "Now go. I have some things I need to do."

"Thank you."

She nodded and led us out, then shut the door quickly behind us.

Grey turned to me. "Let me walk you back."

I nodded, tucking the small book into my pocket.

"You'll read it tonight?" he asked.

"That's my plan. I don't think I could wait any longer."

"I don't blame you. And you found it in the Shadow Guild tower?"

I nodded. "Eve's raven pointed it out to me. Landed on the box and started pecking like its life depended on it."

"That's odd."

As if it had heard us speaking about it, the raven appeared overhead. It flew below the low-hanging clouds, swooping silently through the air. I thought of the seer's words: *find the raven.*

We reached my flat a moment later, and the raven disappeared. I turned to Grey, who stood over me, silhouetted against the moonlight. The glow highlighted his cheekbones and strong jaw, made his silver eyes glitter with warmth.

He was impossibly beautiful, and my gaze moved to his lips.

I wanted to invite him inside. Desperately.

But the book hung heavy in my pocket, a reminder of what was at stake. So much. I needed to focus. If he came up, there'd be only one thing I would pay attention to, and it wouldn't be the book.

I drew in a breath and leaned upward, pressing my lips to his. I kept the kiss chaste, even though desire pounded through me like a stampeding animal. I wanted to pull him against me and feel the heat of him.

"Carrow," he murmured against my lips.

His hands gripped my waist, and I gave in, just a little bit. I raised my hands and clutched at his shoulders, pulling him against me. Heat tore through me as his lips moved expertly on mine.

My thoughts began to blur as I became nothing but feeling. I kissed him like my life depended on it, trying to cram everything I could into that short moment.

A bird's cry distracted me, pulling me from the kiss. I drew back, panting. "This is a bad idea right now. I... can't be around you if I want to read the book."

He nodded, his eyes dark, and stepped back. "Of course. My control is...not what it should be."

"I'll see you tomorrow morning and let you know what I've discovered."

"All right." He nodded and left, and I watched until he disappeared into the night.

Heart still pounding, I looked up, searching for the bird that had ruined the moment. There was something up with that little weirdo, and I needed to figure it out.

I saw nothing but clouds and the moon, so I turned and went inside, taking the stairs two at a time.

As I passed Mac's open door, she shouted out at me, "Any luck with the book?"

I popped my head in and spotted her on the couch with Cordelia, each of them holding a glass of wine. I raised a brow. "You're teaching my raccoon bad habits."

"Ha," Mac said. "She's teaching me."

It's true. Cordelia nodded.

"Well, you two stay out of trouble." I raised the book. "Because Seraphia helped me open it, and I've got some reading to do."

"Excellent!" Mac raised her glass in a toast. "Let me know if you need any help."

"Will do." I eyed them both, putting on my serious face. "Remember what I said. You're both adults. No shenanigans."

"Absolutely no shenanigans," Mac said.

Cordelia kept her mouth shut, but there was a gleam in her eye.

I left them to it, continuing up to my flat. I grabbed a bagel out of the kitchen and didn't even bother to toast it, just shoved a bite in my mouth as I went to the couch. I needed to eat but didn't want to take the time to prepare anything. It was pretty terrible, though.

I flopped on the couch and looked at the book.

A sharp little noise drew my attention to the partially open window.

The raven sat there, staring at me.

The seer had said to find the raven, but the bird was making it easy. "You know, you're getting a bit creepy."

The raven flew over and landed on the cushion next to me, staring down at the book with gleaming black eyes.

"You want me to read it to you?" I asked.

The raven didn't so much as twitch.

I took a huge bite of dust-dry bagel and chewed determinedly as I flipped open the book.

What the hell?

Like before, the writing was nearly indecipherable. Scribbles that didn't look like English. Or any other language I'd ever seen, for that matter.

I held it up to the bird. "Can you read this?"

The bird said nothing. I hadn't really expected it to, but if this new world had taught me anything, it was that you shouldn't underestimate the language capacities of the furred, fanged, or winged.

I began to flip through the book, looking for a language I recognized. I was really only fluent in English, but I could recognize a few more and was willing to type the text into an online translator.

Unfortunately, nothing clicked.

I dug into my pocket and pulled out Rasla's seal.

Holding it up, I looking for a clue in the stone. They'd been stored together, so maybe the seal would help me read the book. I studied the emblem on it. The Celtic design looked nothing like the ones in the book, and his name certainly wasn't helpful. I put the seal back and continued to search the book for anything I recognized.

There was nothing.

Except, that wasn't true. I couldn't read the words, but I could *feel* something in them. It was like my soul was beginning to buzz with energy. A sense of recognition zipped between the book and me, powerful and strange.

Finally, I turned to a page with several twisty, Celtic-looking symbols. I'd never seen anything like them before—not even on Rasla's seal—but they called to me. Fiercely.

Gently, I pressed my fingertips to the page and felt a jolt of energy travel up my arm.

Magic surged within me, both familiar and foreign. It fizzed through my veins, filling my soul with light. Pressure built, an undeniable need to *do something.*

The bird squawked, so close I could touch it.

I *wanted* to touch it.

My fingertips buzzed to press against the smooth feathers, to feed some of my magic into the bird. Instinct drove me—or maybe it was the book, feeding knowledge into my soul. Whatever it was, everything suddenly felt natural. Inevitable.

I kept one hand pressed to the book and raised the other. The bird watched me with wary black eyes, head tilted.

Then it hopped closer.

Shaking, I rested my fingertips against its smooth, ebony feathers. Magic exploded within me, bursting out through my fingertips and into the bird.

Light glowed around the feathered animal, and it squawked loudly. I jerked, nearly removing my hand. But instinct stopped me.

I kept my fingertips pressed to the bird's feathers, letting the magic surge from me into the small creature. The book felt like a conduit or a battery, helping my magic flow with incredible ease and power. I still couldn't read the symbols on the page, but somehow, my soul understood what was happening.

The magic shifted, growing stronger. With it, the bird began to grow. Light glowed from it so brightly that I could no longer see the creature.

The air popped, and power sparked across my skin.

When the light died, the bird was gone.

A person sat next to me.

Beatrix.

Holy fates, it was Beatrix, her red hair gleaming in the light. Shock dropped my stomach to my knees, and I gasped.

My long dead friend...returned?

8

———

Weak from magic use, I stared at the figure on the couch.

Beatrix.

It was her—there was no doubt. Same brilliant red hair, green eyes, pale skin. The same little scar through her brow that she'd got when we'd gone rock climbing in the Peak District, and she'd fallen.

Confusion flickered in her eyes, along with fear. She leapt off the couch, spinning around, her gaze frantic.

"Beatrix?" I rose slowly, my heart thundering a mile a minute. *What the hell had happened?* "Is it really you?"

"Um..." She looked down at her arms, brow creased in concern, then looked up at me. "It is."

"You're not...dead?" My skin chilled. I'd *seen* her body.

"I don't think so?" Confusion echoed in her voice. Her eyes flicked up to mine. "And you're truly here?"

"Yes." I threw my arms around her, thrilled when she felt solid and real.

My magic flared to life, trying to read her the way it always did. In my mind flashed images of the sky and trees from above. From her time as a bird?

She laughed and hugged me back. It felt so good to hug my friend again. It'd been over a year since she'd been murdered by the necromancer's henchman. I'd thought her gone forever.

She winced, pulling back. Pain twisted her features, and she reached up to rub her head.

Concern flared to life inside me. "Are you all right?"

"Um—" She swallowed hard, staggering slightly. "Some memories are coming back. Foggy, though."

"Come." I grabbed her arm and pulled her to the small table near the kitchen. "Sit and have some tea. Get your bearings."

She nodded and sat, looking around with confusion. "This isn't your normal place."

"It's long gone. We're not even really in London anymore."

"Not in London?" She jumped up from the chair and went to the window, staggering slightly. I raced after her, wanting to stop her, to force her to sit and recover, but I couldn't imagine how confused she was. If she wanted to see it for herself, I wouldn't stop her.

And hell, she'd survived death. She'd surely survive a little stumble in my living room. She pushed the window open further, and I realized she was wearing the same clothes she'd died in. The T-shirt had a slogan on the back from a bar we liked: "For a good time, go to Sal's."

Sal's had not been a particularly good time, but we'd both been broke and appreciated a free T-shirt.

She leaned out and looked around. "Holy crap. It's like we've gone back in time."

I joined her and looked out at the steeply peeked roofs, wooden beams, white plaster, and mullioned windows. "Yep. You don't remember it at all?"

She squinted, looking hard at the roofs and clouds. "I do, actually. But mostly from above. I was...a bird? Flying through this city?"

I nodded. "Yeah."

"How is that possible?"

"So you didn't know that magic existed? That you would turn into a bird when you died?" Where the hell did I even start with the questions?

She shook her head. "Magic? As in pulling rabbits out of hats?"

"Not exactly." So Beatrix hadn't been a secret supernatural all along. Not that I'd really thought about it, but how had she turned into a bird? And why was she back?

I brought her back.

The thought flared in my mind. I'd been so excited about her return—about her *survival*—that I'd forgotten I'd used the book and my magic to bring her back.

I'd defied death.

Somehow.

I ran to the couch and picked up the book, flipping through the pages. It was undamaged, thank fates, but I still couldn't read the strange writing. I looked up at Beatrix, who had turned to face me.

"I think I could use that tea now, thanks." She gave a wan smile.

I snapped the book shut. "Coming right up."

My mind raced as I hurried to the kitchen and put the kettle on, then returned to the living room. Beatrix stood near the door, her eyes glued to Cordelia, who had just walked in.

"There's a wild animal in your house," Beatrix said.

Who's she calling wild?

"Calm down, Cordelia. She's new here." I glanced at Beatrix, who looked between the raccoon and me with wide eyes.

"Cordelia?" Beatrix asked.

"That's her name. She arrived at our block of flats shortly after your...death."

Death? Cordelia looked at me with interest.

I *so* did not have the time or ability to explain things

to both of them. Especially since I barely understood what was going on.

"Cordelia, you can have any snack you want if you'll give us a few moments to talk." I looked at Beatrix. "And we're going to get to the bottom of this." I walked to her and gripped her hand. "But I am *so happy* you are here."

She smiled. "Me too. It's been...weird."

"You have no idea. Just give me a moment to get the tea." I released my grip and returned to the kitchen.

Cordelia trundled after me, climbing into the snack cupboard to find something to her fancy. From inside the cupboard, she asked, *Is that Beatrix?*

"Yes. How did you know?"

You talked about her a little with Grey while I eavesdropped.

"Admitting to it so freely?"

She climbed out of the cupboard, a bag of biscuits in her hand, and shrugged. *Also, I think her disappearance was when I knew to come to your house.*

"You think that spurred it on?"

Something had to. Things were changing. Fate was moving the wheel. I could feel it, so I followed it.

"Is that a familiar thing?"

She shrugged. *Maybe.*

With any luck, Beatrix might regain some memories of her time as a raven and have some answers. Because that was some serious magical business. Hopefully, she'd know something.

I finished making the tea—with way too much milk and sugar, just the way Beatrix liked it—and took the mugs to the small table.

She sat, staring at the wood grain, her gaze somewhat vacant. When I appeared in her peripheral vision, she jerked and looked up at me, her eyes clearing.

"Remembering more stuff?" I set the mug on the table.

She nodded. "I spent a lot of time in the air and following a woman around. She had"—she waved her hand around her head—"ever-changing colorful hair."

"Eve."

"That's her name?" She nodded thoughtfully. "That fits. Like Adam and Eve from the garden."

"Not quite." Did I explain now that Eve was Fae?

"Okay, sure. But, I mean, she reminded me of life. And nature. There was, like, a light that glowed around her—an energy that made me feel good. Comforted. Like it kept me from being pulled into the darkness."

"Do you think the darkness was...death?"

"Maybe." She sipped her tea, thinking. "I honestly have no idea, but it felt like she was helping to keep me near you. I could feel you, and that's where I wanted to be. What's going on?"

"Well..." I didn't actually have an answer to that, but I could start at the beginning. "You know my weird ability to see things?"

"Yeah."

"It's magic. Not rabbit-in-the-hat magic, but real magic." As quickly as I could, I filled her in on everything that had happened after her death: me, my magic, coming to Guild City, meeting Mac and the rest of the gang. Grey.

Occasionally, she looked over at Cordelia, who had finished off her biscuits and sat clutching the empty bag.

Finally, I finished my tale, or as much of it as I thought was relevant.

"Holy crap." Beatrix looked down at her now cold tea. "You're serious?"

"Totally."

She drew in a deep breath. "That's amazing."

"Wait until you see the city."

"I don't know if I'll be able to handle it."

"You will. I'm sure."

She nodded. "I hope so. I guess it all makes a weird kind of sense. I wasn't fully myself. I just knew that the woman—Eve—felt good to be around. Then, when you arrived, it was like I'd been waiting for you. Time passed, and you became more and more familiar to me, like my memory was returning."

"And that's why you turned up the other morning and took me to the Shadow Guild tower and showed me where the book was."

"Yes!" Her eyes flashed with the excitement of memory. "That day, it was like all the pieces were falling into place. I knew you would save me, and that the answers were there."

"Was it my magic that would save you?"

"It had to be, right? This whole place runs on magic, from what it sounds like."

"That's true." And I had been coming into my power more and more.

"I could feel your power growing," she said. "It made you more familiar to me. Like I was tied to you. Like I'd *been* tied to you since the moment I died, but I didn't remember until you gained more of your magic."

"And Eve?"

"She helped, somehow. Her power kept me on this plane until you showed up."

I leaned back in the chair. "I truly have no explanation for this."

Beatrix shrugged. "Well, I think you saved me."

I laughed weakly. I *wanted* that to be true. Not only because I didn't want her to disappear again, but because maybe that was my secret power. Maybe I could save people from death.

Maybe I could save Grey from death.

A knock sounded on my door—two fast, one slow, distinctly Mac—and then it pushed open. She stood in the doorway, staring at Beatrix and me.

"Why is Eve's raven suddenly a person?" she asked.

"You can tell?" I said.

"Don't you feel it?" Mac pointed to Beatrix. "Her signature is just like the raven's."

I hadn't noticed, actually. I'd been so shocked over her arrival. But she was right. The air around her felt like a howling wind, thin in my lungs. It'd been such a faint signature when associated with the raven that I hadn't consciously noticed it. but I did now. It was extremely faint, but definitely there.

"I'm not a bird," Beatrix said.

"Nope, you're definitely not." Mac strode over and held out her hand. "I'm Macbeth O'Connell."

"That's quite a name." Beatrix grinned and held out her hand. "I'm Beatrix."

"Beatrix?" Mac's brows rose and she turned to me. "*The* Beatrix? Beatrix of the books?"

"The very same," I said.

"You're not dead," Mac said.

"Apparently not." Beatrix looked at me. "You still have my books?"

"Only thing I have from our old life."

Beatrix scowled. "I guess all my stuff is gone, huh?"

"Long gone."

"Damn."

"What's the deal?" Mac said.

"I might have brought her back from the dead somehow."

Mac's brows rose. "Really? Do you think it was the necromancer magic you absorbed from the crystal?"

"*What*, now?" Beatrix asked.

I hadn't thought of that. "I don't know. I absorbed magic from the necromancer's crystal after Beatrix's death. But by then, she was already a raven."

"Good point. It must be a power you inherently have." Mac tapped her chin. "But what the hell sort of power is it?"

"I don't know." I raised the book. "And I think there should be answers in here, but I can't read it."

Mac held out her hand, and I passed it over. She flipped open the book and studied it. "Hmm. Did Seraphia look in here?"

"No. She helped me unlock it, but by then, it was late, so I took it home to read."

"We need to take it back to her."

"Who is Seraphia?" Beatrix asked.

I realized I'd left her out—I'd probably left a lot out—and I quickly explained.

Mac leaned forward. "You know what? Why don't I hang out with Beatrix? Help her get adjusted to Guid City. Maybe figure out her magic. And that will give you time to get to the bottom of this book."

Beatrix nodded. "That sounds like a good idea. You have a lot at stake, don't you?"

"So much."

Beatrix gripped my hand. "That settles it, then. I'll hang out with my new friend here, and I'll be around if you need me." She hiked a thumb toward my couch.

"That's my new bed, by the way. The raccoon is going to have to share."

I laughed. "Thank you."

"No, *thank you.* Because I'm pretty sure I'd be dead without you."

"Maybe. I don't know. I need to figure it out." I looked down at the book, wishing I could read it. There was so much I didn't know. If I'd really brought Beatrix back...how had I done it?

Exhaustion tugged at me. I'd been going nonstop since I'd found the book and gone to Transylvania. I needed a nap of the eight-hour variety.

Aching, I stood. "Let's get ready for bed. Tomorrow, we'll figure this out."

Between the two of us, Mac and I had enough extra bedding to make Beatrix a place on the sofa. Cordelia vacated it for the chair near the window, though she might eventually move into my room.

As I went to my bedroom, I turned to look back at my friend, already tucked into her couch bed.

Beatrix.

She was back.

How was I so lucky?

"Night," Beatrix said.

"Night." I waved, then went to my room. My mind raced as I settled down into bed, and it was impossible not to think of Grey.

Could I save him like I'd saved Beatrix?

9

____

G*REY*

The dream was both heaven and hell. It pulled at me. Carrow on one side, the afterlife on the other. The flames of the underworld flickered, trying to drag me toward them. It was a place of myth and legend. Though I'd never been to an underworld, my perception of it was as old as I was—a place of torture, where I'd pay for the sins of my past.

In the present, on Earth, there was Carrow.

And yet, I couldn't have both her and life.

I woke, sweating and gasping.

Fates, I was a disaster.

Embarrassing.

I swung myself out of bed and drew in a bracing breath. Everything felt heavier, as it had since the curse had come back into effect. My mortality dragged at me in wakefulness and in sleep, with every second ticking by and moving me closer to an unacceptable future. I could feel time like it was a physical thing.

I shook away the thought and headed for the shower. I was due to meet Carrow soon. Next to her was the only place I wanted to be. My previous self would consider the thought insane, but I'd accepted it.

She'd changed me. Massively so.

Though part of me struggled with the idea, the rest didn't give a damn. I wanted to be by her side. Now, in the future, forever.

I prayed the book had taught her something that would help us, because the visit to the seer had not been as promising as I'd hoped. I'd put on a good face for Carrow, but the results of that visit had been disappointing. True, we'd learned a great deal of new information, but it had laid the entire task on Carrow's shoulders, and I hated it. This should be my burden.

Quickly, I showered and dressed, choosing one of my usual suits without thinking. I drank a liter of bagged blood to give myself strength, grimacing at the stale taste. It was nothing like Carrow, but I couldn't risk it.

Ready, I left the flat and passed Miranda's desk with a brief farewell. The morning was brisk as I walked toward Carrow's flat. Supernaturals were out and about, headed for work and play.

Near Carrow's flat, I passed a coffeehouse. The aroma wafted out onto the street, rich and enticing. I turned in to pick up a coffee for her. There was no time to waste, but there was also no need to be uncivilized.

Having no idea who I would find at Carrow's flat, I ordered four coffees. The clerk arranged them in a small cardboard carrier, and I headed back out into the morning.

As I neared Carrow's flat, I caught sight of someone looking at me from across the street. I stared back, trying to place him, but it was just an unfamiliar young man, looking at me with surprise. There wasn't a hint of threat coming from him, but he was staring at...

Me. He was staring at *me*, carrying a tray of coffees like a common errand boy. I felt my eyebrows rise and a slight, silent laugh escape my throat.

If some of my enemies could see me now.

Carrow had...domesticated me.

It was vaguely uncomfortable, but not unbearable.

But now was not the time for insufferable navel gazing. I'd done enough of that already. I turned toward her green door and knocked loudly, then looked up at the flats above.

Mac leaned out of her window and stared down at me, her pale hair tousled. Her gaze landed on the coffees. "Is one of those for me?"

"Certainly."

She nodded. "Be right there."

A moment later, her footsteps pounded down the stairs. She could give a rhinoceros a run for its money. The door swung open, and she reached out to grab a coffee. "Thanks."

I nodded. "Of course."

She raised an eyebrow. "Of course? The Devil of Darkvale is an *of course I deliver coffee* sort of man?"

"I suppose not, but it seemed like the appropriate thing to say."

She shrugged. "Fair enough. Come on up. Carrow has a surprise for you."

Excitement thrilled through me. Had she found a solution? "Of what sort?"

"You'll just have to wait and see." She turned and took the stairs two at a time.

I followed her to the top floor, turning right to follow her into Carrow's small flat. It was as charming as usual, save for the unfamiliar woman sitting on the couch, a pale redhead. Anxiety radiated from her, along with curiosity. Her green eyes raced over the entire space, including me, taking everything in like she was a person from outer space.

There was something familiar about her, too. Her magical signature reminded me of another's. But whose?

Carrow came out of the kitchen, dressed in her usual attire of dark jeans and a simple shirt. Her hair glowed golden around her head, and her beauty took me away.

The newcomer was forgotten, and I held out the coffee tray. "For you."

Her gaze landed on it, warming. "Thank you."

I nodded.

She approached, and I held my breath, not wanting to risk inhaling her miraculous scent.

She took the tray and removed one coffee, handing it to me. Then she turned toward the oddly familiar woman and handed her a coffee. "Try this."

"Thanks." The woman took the coffee, her gaze moving back to me.

From behind, footsteps sounded on the stairs. I turned, spotting Eve. The Fae rushed into the room, her hair brilliant blue today. Curiosity gleamed in her eyes, and her dress looked wrinkled and worn. Two different shoes adorned her feet.

"Well, don't you look a sight." Mac grinned. "In a hurry this morning?"

"Give me a break." Eve strode into the room, her gaze on the new woman. "You're supposed to be the raven?"

The raven?

"I—" The newcomer shrugged, her face utterly confused. "Apparently so, yes."

I turned to Carrow. "What is happening?"

"You're never going to believe this." Carrow held up a finger, a contrite expression on her face. "But just give me a half a second?"

"Of course."

I stepped back against the wall. A drama was about to unfold. If I'd learned anything in my long life, it was how to sense tension. And the air was loaded with it.

Carrow looked at Eve. "This is Beatrix. She's spent the last year as the raven that followed you. You really couldn't see her?"

Her old friend Beatrix? The one that had been murdered?

Eve sighed. "I could see her, all right? I just didn't want to talk about it."

"Why?" Carrow asked.

"We all have secrets, Carrow." Eve folded her arms. "Until now, this didn't matter. And honestly, I'm not even sure *what* any of it means."

"Try," Carrow said. "Please. Because as far as I knew, Beatrix was dead. But..."

"I'm not." The newcomer shrugged, confusion flickering in her gaze. "I died, and I felt it. Horrible." She shuddered. "But then something happened, and I woke up with you. Or at least, near you. I felt your presence like a light. Like something that kept me on this plane."

Eve crossed her arms, clutching her biceps tightly. Indecision flickered in her eyes, along with a bit of fear. "I've got some magic I don't quite understand. Something Fae, but I don't have a Court, so I've never learned what it is."

"A Court?" Beatrix frowned.

"Beatrix has no idea about the magical world," said Carrow, then turned to Beatrix. "And I promise, I'll explain it all later."

Beatrix nodded, frowning slightly. This had to be a lot for her to take in.

Eve continued. "I knew you were following me, but you never spoke. And you never acted like much more than an overly familiar bird. So I assumed it was just some kind of Snow White affinity for animals. But since it wasn't dangerous, I decided to ignore it. I like my life the way it is, and I know that if I poke into my Fae ancestry, I might find something I don't like."

"It's not just you," Beatrix said. "It's Carrow, too. She's the one who drew me the strongest. I think she's the one who kept me from dying. I could feel her presence. Her energy. She yanked me back from the brink of death, but you were like an energy source that kept me here. So I followed you."

Eve nodded, her eyes flickering with worry. She looked like she wanted to ask Beatrix to stop talking. Or perhaps like she would run from the room. Instead, she said, "Well, I'm pleased that I could help you."

Beatrix grinned ruefully. "Me, too. I wasn't ready to die."

Carrow smiled, seeming satisfied. "Thank you, Eve. I was dying to hear what you know about this."

"Not much, I'm afraid," Eve said. "I don't know anything more than that."

"Neither do I." Carrow looked at me. "But I think this has to do with us. I think I can use this to save you."

I frowned, completely lost. "You're going to need to elaborate, because I cannot see the connection."

Carrow went to the table and picked up the small book that Seraphia had unlocked yesterday. "This book ignited something in my magic. It allowed me to bring Beatrix back from the dead."

"But how?" None of this made any sense.

As I listened, she told a story of using the book to control her magic in a way that allowed her to help Beatrix transition from raven to human. "But what I don't understand is how she went from dead girl to raven," she concluded. "And how that might apply to you."

That was a definite gap in the story. I looked at Beatrix. "Are you a supernatural?"

"They tell me that I am." She pointed to Carrow and Mac. "But I don't know what kind."

I looked at Carrow. "Is her signature strong?"

"It's thready," she said. "Like it's there, but struggling."

Slowly, so as not to startle her, I approached Beatrix. "May I touch your hand? I am gifted with an excellent sense for reading magical signatures."

"Um, sure..." Discomfort flickered across her face, but she held out her hand.

I rested mine over hers gently, feeling the faintest

pulse of magic through her. It felt like a howling wind, high up in the atmosphere. Even the air that I breathed began to feel thin.

Beyond it, though...

Beyond it, I felt Carrow.

My gaze flicked to Carrow. "Did you sense your own signature on her?"

"No." Confusion flashed on her face. "I felt a powerful wind, and the air was thin in my lungs, but there was nothing of mine."

"But there is." I focused more intently on Beatrix's magic. "Deep in her soul, there is a small part of you. I can feel it. There's no doubt that it is your magic."

"Really?" Carrow approached.

I removed my hand from Beatrix's and stepped back. Carrow raised her own hand. "Do you mind?"

Beatrix shook her head, and Carrow touched her shoulder. She closed her eyes and focused. Seconds passed, then a minute. Her eyes opened, and she removed her hand. "Maybe I feel it. It's hard to say."

"Well, I think I feel it," Beatrix said. "Like you're with me. It's what drew me to you while I was still a raven and didn't have my memory."

Carrow turned to me. "This is the mystery that I want to get to the bottom of. If I could do this for her, then maybe I can do it for you."

"Break the curse?"

She shrugged. "Maybe. I don't understand *how* it

could work. I just know that it could. And that this book"—she raised it—"has answers."

"Did you read it all?"

"I couldn't." She flipped it open and showed me.

The text was indecipherable. More like tiny images of intricate shapes—not a language I'd ever seen.

"The whole thing is like this," she said. "I want to take it back to Seraphia."

"We'll do that now." I looked at her, unsure of how any of this would work. Were we even on the right path? My dream had made it clear that our time was short, and the afterworld beckoned.

10

CARROW

I looked at Beatrix, wondering what to do with her while Grey and I sought answers. She looked confused and worried. Mac had kindly offered to keep her company, but it seemed unfair to leave her here while there was so much outside my small flat. And I missed my friend.

"Want to see a bit of the city?" I asked.

Beatrix nodded, her expression lightening. "Yeah. I suppose I need to sort my life out, now that I have it back."

"We'll figure it out," I said, unable to help looking back at Grey.

I could feel Beatrix watching the two of us, her radar going wild. She'd been my friend for so long that she knew when I liked a guy. And what I felt for Grey was far from something so simple and juvenile as *like.*

I grabbed my jacket and the book, making sure that Rasla's seal was inside the jacket pocket. Together, we left the flat. At the street, Eve veered off for her shop, looking back twice at Beatrix, her brow creased with concern. There were hidden depths to Eve, and I was glad she'd felt comfortable enough to admit what she had.

Now we just needed to figure out my exact role and how I could use my strange skills to help Grey.

Mac, clever genius that she was, stuck close to Beatrix, pointing out the different sights around town. I remembered my first days there. My old friend would be having a hard time falling asleep tonight. Mac's actions gave Grey and me a bit of privacy, and he joined me, walking close by my side.

"Thank you for the coffee," I said.

"My pleasure." He looked down at the book. "You truly think you have the ability to break the curse?"

"Yes." I could feel it. "Or at least, I have the ability to fix our situation. I don't know how, but my magic is screaming it. If only Seraphia can help decipher the book."

We reached the library a few moments later.

Unlike the last times we'd visited, Seraphia was loitering outside the front door. She looked like she'd recently showered and put on fresh clothes, and her eyes looked well rested. She clutched a mug of tea and stared up at the clouds.

"She seems a bit more herself," I said.

Grey nodded.

Seraphia caught sight of us and smiled. "How was the book?"

"Unexpected." I stopped in front of her and removed it from my pocket. "It's written in a language I don't recognize."

"Really?" She frowned. "I'd have assumed it would be English, given where you found it."

"Me, too. But it's not." I opened it and showed her the strange scribblings. "Check it out. The writing is insane."

She squinted at it, then gasped, her grip loosening on her mug. The ceramic cup slipped from her fingers, and Grey reached down, snagging it before it hit the ground.

"No way," she breathed, reaching for the book with a trembling hand. I let her have it, and she raised it to her face. Quickly, carefully, she flipped through the pages, her jaw slackening. "I've never seen one of these before."

"What is it?" I could feel Mac and Beatrix crowding close.

"Just a moment, and I'll confirm my suspicions." She turned and hurried into the library.

We followed, Beatrix gasping upon entrance. Seraphia raced to her worktable, winding her way through the shelves, and we hurried after her. She bent over the table, laying the book out flat and opening it to a random page. Quickly, she ducked under the table and disappeared.

I bent down to peer underneath, then spotted her opening a secret compartment set into the floor.

"I trust you," she said. "Or you'd never see this."

With a few deft maneuvers, she lifted up one of the wooden floorboards, and her hand trembled as she withdrew a box. The ornately carved wood gleamed with the patina of careful care. Quickly, she climbed out from under the table and set the box on the surface.

"Keep an eye on that," she said, then disappeared between some shelves. Her voice drifted back. "I'll only be a moment."

I shared a look with the others, but before we could speak, she'd already returned, a key clutched in her hand. She slipped the key into the box, twisting it carefully. The lid popped open.

Carefully, she removed a stone from the box. It looked average enough, and I frowned. "What's that?"

"Shh." She hovered the stone right over the pages, standing so perfectly still that she was obviously holding her breath. The stone glowed gold, and she heaved a sigh. "Amazing."

"What is it?" I leaned closer, trying to see whatever it was that she could see.

But nothing had changed about the book. It was still indecipherable.

"This isn't quite a book. Not in the way you are used to." She pointed to the words. "And this isn't another language. It was written in English."

"So it's code?"

"Not exactly. It's a spell. The book was written in English, and then enchanted so that the reader could go back in time to visit the events that were written about."

"You're kidding."

"I'm not." She looked up, her face bright with excitement. "These books are incredibly rare. We had several in our collection, but they were stolen ages ago. This is the first I've ever seen with my own eyes."

"How do we use it, then?" I asked.

"Come, I'll show you." She turned, leading us deeper into the library. We wound our way between shelves, getting lost in the recesses of the cavernous building. It grew darker and gloomier, the air chilling.

Finally, we reached a section of bookshelves that appeared empty. The wooden shelves formed a narrow aisle that led into the darkness. A faint glitter filled the air between the shelves, and I stepped toward it.

Seraphia reached out and gripped my arm. "Stop."

I halted immediately, staring at the space with rapt attention.

"The library no longer has any of those books," she said. "But we still have our portal. If you carry the book between those shelves, you'll be taken back in time to whenever the book was written."

"For real, back in time?" Beatrix asked, skepticism in her voice.

I couldn't help but feel the same. I'd seen amazing things in the magical world, but time travel?

"Yes." Seraphia nodded. "You'll arrive in this very library, but in the past."

"Likely in the time of Rasla," I said, suddenly feeling Beatrix's confusion. I turned to her. "Around 1642. He was a bastard, but it's a very long story."

"I can tell you over breakfast," Mac said.

I looked at Seraphia. "So I can take this book and go back to get my answers?"

She nodded. "Yes. But I don't know what you'll find. And it will be dangerous."

I'd seen enough movies to know that. Time travel was no joke. "Once I'm there, how do I know what I'm looking for?"

Seraphia frowned slightly. "From what I understand, certain scenes or people might glow with magic. A golden sparkle or faint aura. Those are the things that are written about in the book. Theoretically, at least. You're going to have to wing it, for the most part. Your magic should help, though."

I thought of the dress the book had been wrapped in and the image of the woman I'd seen when I'd touched it. We needed to find her. "When it's all done, how do I come home?"

"Return to the portal. It will remember you and send you here."

"What if the library is destroyed?" I asked, mind racing.

She grimaced. "You may be stuck. I'm not sure."

I looked at Grey. "Worth the risk, don't you think?"

"Of course. I will accompany you."

"More people might be more dangerous," Seraphia said.

"I lived in Guild City in the mid-seventeenth century," he said. "She'll need my help."

"That's true," I said. "I have no idea how to get along back then. And who knows what we'll find? We're doing this to fix our situation, so it's better if we stay together."

"Fair enough," Seraphia said. "And it's not my place to tell you what to do. But it is my place to warn you. Do not change anything. Just observe. Blend in. People will be able to see you."

I nodded. "I know the drill. I mean, I learned it from TV and movies, but I assume all the same rules apply?"

Seraphia nodded. "From what I know, yes."

"We'll need a good plan," Grey said. "I shouldn't see my former self. But it would be good to make use of my resources in the past."

I nodded, liking the idea of having a place to stay.

"Don't forget about clothes," Beatrix said. "You'd stick out like a sore thumb in those."

We'd need potions too, certainly. Things to help us along when things got sticky. I looked at my friends. "All right. Let's get moving."

Hours later, we were ready. Grey and I had come up with a plan with the help of the others, and then Beatrix and Mac had gone to Eve to get the potions we would need. Grey and I had headed over to the Fae dress shop. The proprietor had connections with the antique costuming community, and we'd found proper attire for the seventeenth century.

I pulled at the bodice of my heavy black dress. We'd gone as simple as possible, as far as fashion was concerned, but the skirt was still wide and the three-quarter-length sleeves full. The dress exposed much of my shoulders, though we'd topped it with a cape. It was enchanted like my other dresses had been, giving me a bit of extra strength and protection.

The plan was for me to blend in as a possible acquaintance of Grey's. He was meant to be himself, though we'd have to deal with the past version of him, which would take some doing.

We stood in the library, just the two of us in the small waiting room at the side. Seraphia was off doing something else, and Mac and Beatrix hadn't arrived yet. I looked over at him, attired in all black—breeches, tall boots, and a doublet that looked a bit like a stiff, formal jacket. He held a wide-brimmed hat that he would put on when we arrived. It wasn't his usual look, but it wasn't bad, either. "I can't believe you ever got rid of your old clothes."

He gave me a perplexed look. "I'm hardly the sentimental type. And we're lucky that ruffs had gone out of fashion by the time that book was written."

I laughed at the idea of him in a tall, fancy collar. He didn't wear a wig, though they had been popular then. He never had, apparently.

The door to the library creaked open, and I looked out, spotting Mac and Beatrix. Mac held up a leather bag. "Got your potions."

"Thank you." I stepped out of the small waiting room and saw Beatrix more fully.

Her eyes were wide and sparkling as they met mine. "This place is phenomenal."

"Glad you like it, because you need to live here now that all of London thinks you're dead. I have no idea how you'd get along back there."

"That's fine with me." She looked down at her hands, her brow furrowed as if she expected to see something there. "I just wish I knew if I had magic."

"You do," Mac said. "You turned into a raven, for fates' sake."

"That could have been Carrow," Beatrix said.

"Nah." Mac shook her head. "Her magic did something to you when you died, that's for sure. But I doubt it turned you into a raven."

I nodded. "That's my bet, too."

Seraphia appeared from the back of the library, her hair a bit messy from whatever she'd been getting into. "Ready?"

I cut my eyes to Grey, who nodded. "Looks like it."

"Good." She gestured for us to follow, then turned around. "You're going to want to be as quick as possible. The longer you stay, the more dangerous it will be. And whatever you do, don't lose that book."

I nodded, clutching it tightly. The Fae seamstress had sewn a special pocket into my heavy skirts for it, and I tucked it in, buttoning the pocket closed. I also had Rasla's seal, though I had no idea what to do with it.

The library grew darker and quieter the deeper back we went, until finally, we stood in front of the empty aisle. The air sparkled with pale golden light, beckoning.

"Be careful," Beatrix said. "Being dead sucks."

I cracked a smile and looked at Grey.

He held out a hand.

I took it, unable to help the faint shiver that ran up my arm, filling me with heat. Together, we stepped toward the light. Magic pulled at me, sparking against my skin. Nerves fluttered in my stomach, my breath growing short.

The magic tugged harder the deeper we went. I pulled the book from my pocket, hoping that the portal could tell where we wanted to go.

"Open the book," Seraphia said from behind us.

Carefully, I flipped it open with one hand, choosing a page at random. I couldn't read any of the pages, so I figured it didn't matter which one I opened to.

The lights around us glowed more brightly, the magic pulsing. It yanked at me, pulling me into the ether and spinning me through space. I gripped Grey's hand tightly, terrified of losing him.

My head whirled and my stomach pitched as we traveled, my vision going dark. Finally, hard ground appeared beneath my feet, and I stumbled. Grey caught me, pulling me against him.

Panting, I opened my eyes.

We stood in the library. It was even darker than it had been before, the golden light faint.

"Did it work?" I whispered.

"I think so."

We left the aisle, moving silently. What would the librarian think if she saw us? Would she know we'd come from another time?

The main part of the library wasn't quite as empty as it was in our era. Several patrons strolled through the aisles, their clothing ornate and heavy-looking, just like ours.

I looked up at Grey, noticing that he had put his hat on and tilted his head down. He needed to remain unnoticed until we'd taken care of his past self. Two Devils of Darkvale walking around town would be problematic.

We ducked back into the aisle, and I reached into my bag, pulling out one of the face-altering potions Eve had given us. It wouldn't change our looks much, and it wouldn't work for long, but it would make him slightly unrecognizable as the Devil if one were to only glance at him. We hadn't wanted to use it unless necessary, but the library was busy at this hour.

I handed it to him, and he drank it. His face shifted only slightly—becoming slightly broader and his hair paler—but it was enough that he'd probably go unrecognized.

"That worked well," I said.

"Good. Let's check out the tower."

I nodded and followed him through the library, trying not to make contact. Near the door, a woman stepped into our path. She wore a pitch-black dress like mine, though far more severe and high-collared. Her eyes glinted with suspicion.

"I did not see you enter." Her tone was cold and quiet.

Grey inclined his head politely. "You were turned away at the time."

She frowned, inspecting us. My heart fluttered. Just because the library had the portal didn't mean that all librarians approved of its use.

"If you will allow us to pass, we would be greatly indebted to you," Grey said, his voice vibrating with his power.

The woman's eyes unfocused, his magic forcing her will, and she nodded, stepping aside.

He strode past her, pulling me along. I hurried to keep up, and we stepped out onto the streets of Guild city in the middle of a dreary, cloudy day.

"Whoa." The word slipped out on a breath. "This is different."

The street was lit by magical lamps, the contents of the shop windows not terribly different than in the modern day. Supernaturals still roamed the streets, but their clothing was so stiff and staid compared to what I was used to. Horses filled the streets, pulling narrow carriages. According to Mac, they'd fallen out of favor when motorbikes had become popular, and probably because they smelled. In fact, the whole town bore a stench.

"It stinks here," I whispered.

"Hardly." A wry smile tugged at the corner of Grey's mouth. "We used magic to manage the waste and odor.

It was not quite as good as the plumbing that replaced it, but far better than what the humans dealt with."

I nodded. "If you say so."

"Come, we will check the Shadow Guild tower."

I nodded and followed him down the street. It was the first part of our plan, because it was the best way to know where we were, temporally speaking. Had Rasla hidden the tower yet? Did people here know of the Shadow Guild, or had he already erased it from their memories?

We moved swiftly through the small crowd, darting into a back alley as soon as we reached one. I could still navigate easily enough, but the differences in the city made it a slightly odd experience.

Within minutes, we reached the part of town where the tower stood. I stepped out of the alley and into the empty square, staring at the flat section of wall.

"He's already done it." I shook my head. "The tower is gone."

"It's truly incredible how he managed it." Disgust echoed in Grey's voice.

I looked at the quiet square. There were no weeds yet, just carefully placed gravel made of pale brown stones. The statue of Rasla stood in the middle, unencumbered by weeds. All around, the shops stared silently out at the empty space. Only half of them were closed, unlike in the present day, when they were all abandoned. A small boy swept the street outside of one, and Grey strode to him.

He crouched down, and the boy stepped back warily. Grey reached into his pocket and withdrew a small coin, holding it out to show the boy. It was money from this period, obtained from Grey's private collection.

"This is yours if you can tell me what you know about this place." Grey gestured to the empty square and the section of empty wall.

The boy looked from the coin to the square, confusion in his eyes. "Tell you what about it?"

"Anything at all. Does it seem strange to you? Like it has recently changed?"

The boy shrugged. "It's just an empty square. Bad luck there's no guild tower here or business would be better, me mam says."

"Bad luck?"

He nodded, but confusion flickered in his eyes. "Just never been a tower here. Strange, that. But it's the way it's always been."

"What about that statue?" Grey pointed to the stone Rasla. "When did that appear?"

The boy's eyes brightened. "Just the other day. Big ceremony, and we sold rivers of beer."

"Thank you, lad." Grey handed him the coin and stood, then returned to me. "That's that, then. It was recent."

I nodded. "Shall we go to your place?"

"Yes. I'm not sure how much longer this potion will hold." He rubbed his jaw.

Together, we slipped down the alley and back onto the main streets. We moved quickly through the crowd, avoiding people as best we could. The streets had filled more, the evening arriving with a biting chill to the air. As the sun set behind the clouds, the night grew dark. More streetlamps flared to life, magic filling their globes and casting a glow on the people crowding the lanes.

We were nearly to Grey's side of town when a man stepped out of a shop, bumping into me. I stumbled, and he grabbed my arm, trying to keep me from falling.

A shock of discomfort flashed through me at his touch, his magic sick and dark. I looked up, startled.

Right into the face of Councilor Rasla.

11

———

Carrow

He looked just like the statue, with a heavy brow and long nose. But it was his magic I recognized. Evil. Reeking of decay and death.

My heart thundered as Councilor Rasla studied me with shocked eyes. His voice was cold as he demanded, "Who are you?"

"No one of interest to you." I wanted to yank my arm away, but this was too good an opportunity to miss. I used my power, calling it up from within me. It resisted at first, then finally flared to life.

What is going on with you? How do we find out?

An image came to mind—a woman, her face broad and wind-chapped. She held a mop in one hand and a bucket in the other. Brilliant blue eyes stared back at me. The image disappeared.

"Tell me, girl. You look familiar. Who are you?" he demanded.

Familiar? I yanked my arm away, scowling. "No one, sir."

Grey stepped between me and Rasla. "You will leave us be."

His voice echoed with power, and I peeked around his shoulder at Rasla. The man's eyes weren't really going foggy—not as much as a person's eyes normally did when Grey used his power.

Rasla shook his head, trying to drive off the influence of Grey's voice. "You're familiar, girl, and I want to know who you are." His gaze moved to Grey. "And you... there's something about you."

From behind, I could see the tips of Grey's hair changing from light to dark. The spell was wearing off, and his face was returning to normal.

Damn it. We needed to get out of here.

"Forget us." Grey's voice rumbled with power.

Rasla's eyes fogged slightly, but he shook his head violently.

Grey gripped my arm, and we strode away. I looked behind, spotting Rasla staring after us, his face twisted in confusion. He didn't follow us, however.

"That's going to be a problem," Grey murmured.

"He'll look for us."

"I believe so. My power did not work on him this time. Not well, at least. I am not sure why. He may have taken a potion to protect himself from that sort of influence. Or perhaps he's wearing a charm."

I shivered, hoping we could get in and out of there before Rasla caused us too many problems. "He couldn't have recognized me because the last time he saw me, it was in the future. And he was a ghost."

"But he said you looked familiar."

I thought of the woman I'd seen in my vision. Her image had been blurry, but she might have looked like me. Did I remind him of her? "He might have noticed your glamour wearing off."

Grey nodded, his brow furrowed. "We just need to finish and get back to our time before he finds us."

We reached the clearing in front of Grey's tower a moment later, but he stopped, inspecting the guards out front.

"Do you remember them?" I asked.

He shook his head. "Not well. Perhaps not at all. I may be confusing them with others. There have been many over the years."

It sounded terribly lonely.

"We shouldn't enter that way." He pointed toward the side of the tower. "That will be safer. I have a secret entrance. It'd be a shame to run into my former self in front of witnesses, especially with the potion wearing off."

I looked up at him. He was right. He looked almost normal now, back to his usual self. "Pull your hat down further."

He did, dipping his face. "Come."

I followed him around the side of the square, keeping to the front of the restaurants and shops that surrounded his tower. There were trees planted along the city wall, and we were able to stay behind them as we walked, taking advantage of a bit of cover.

The guards looked our way at one point, and Grey waved at them. They inclined their head in recognition, and we continued on.

"They are used to me approaching from this direction," he said. "As long as my former self doesn't walk out those doors in the next two minutes, we'll be fine."

My heartbeat thundered as we neared the tower. Worry streaked through me.

There were *two* Greys in this timeline. Would we be able to manage this bit smoothly? So much rested on it.

We reached the side of the tower, which was concealed behind a grove of trees and flowering rosebushes.

"I had these planted," Grey murmured, "to provide cover for this side entrance."

"Do you still use it?"

"Not as much, no." He stopped in front of the stone wall. There was no door, but he pressed his palm to the stones. Magic flared, and the wall disappeared. A wooden door revealed itself, and he pulled it open and looked inside. "Clear." He stepped into the darkened hallway, and I followed.

The air smelled faintly of candle wax and perfume. Sconces along the hall, lit by magic, glittered gold and green.

Grey gestured to them. "We used that instead of electricity for the longest time."

"Why did you switch?" I quite liked the magical lamps.

"They aren't as convenient as modern lights. Nor as bright."

He was right. The shadows were thick. He started down the hall, gesturing for me to follow. "Come. I spent quite a bit of time in the club during this century. We should check there first."

"The club?"

"Before it was a bar, my tower was a club for the wealthiest and most powerful in town. A bit like a bar, but staider."

I crossed my fingers, hoping we would find the old version of Grey in his flat. It would be easiest to take care of him there.

The noise of the club grew louder as we approached, but we saw no one in the hall. We reached a narrow door, and Grey stopped beside it, whispering, "This hallway is mine alone, but beyond that door is the club."

He reached for a small painting on the wall and

gripped the side of the frame. He pulled, and the painting swung open like a door.

A square piece of murky glass was inset into the wall, and he pressed a hand to it. Suddenly, the smoke in the glass cleared, and an image of the bar on the other side appeared.

"Amazing." I stepped forward, peering into the club.

The structure was the same as it had been in our time, but the stage was gone. The bar was smaller and located on a different wall. Tables of varying sizes were filled with men and women. A mixed gender club must be unusual for the time, but Guild City played by different rules than the real world. Armchairs were positioned in front of flickering fireplaces that no longer existed in the present.

I searched the faces for Grey, hoping not to see him.

When my gaze landed on the impossibly handsome man sitting at a raised table in the corner, my heart raced. Excitement. Fear. "You're in there."

Grey cupped my shoulder, and I looked up at him.

"You're sure you want to try it this way?" Concern echoed in his voice. "I was a different man then. Dangerous."

"You were dangerous when I first met you."

A wry smile tugged at the corner of his mouth. "Perhaps more dangerous now, given our circumstances."

"You would never hurt me."

Darkness flickered in his eyes, along with worry, and I knew he was thinking about the beast inside him.

I pressed a hand to his chest. "Leave it to me. We planned this, and I know what to do."

We'd discussed it a dozen times, the various scenarios that might play out and how we would react. This had been one of them. I stood on tiptoe and pressed a kiss to his mouth, then opened a vial of one of Eve's potions. It was similar to the one he'd taken—a draught that would change my face and even my magical signature.

Grey didn't remember meeting me in the past, and it would be dangerous if his past self sensed that I was his mate. Better for my looks and magic to be different. It would provide me with cover.

I showed Grey my new face. "How do I look?"

"Beautiful. Not as beautiful as normal, but he'll want you."

"How do you know?"

"I know."

"All right, then." I glanced down at my hair, noticing that it was now black. I wouldn't have long with this new face, so I needed to get a move on. "I'll see you soon."

He nodded. "Be careful."

"Will do." I turned and looked through the glass window.

The Grey in the club was looking away and wouldn't

see me enter, so I took my chance and pushed my way through the door, slipping into the crowd.

Immediately, I was surrounded by the scents and sounds of the past, all of it so unfamiliar. The scents were intense—perfumes that had fallen out of favor and strong liquor and wine. The dialect was possible to understand, though difficult.

I drew in a steady breath and approached Grey's table.

The Devil.

I shouldn't think of him as Grey, because he wasn't.

As I neared his table, his gaze landed on me. It was cold—icily so.

Immediately, I was thrown back to when I'd met him for the first time in Guild City. He'd reminded me of a statue carved of the coldest granite. His eyes were an icy gray, his cheekbones sharp, and his jaw hard. As with before, the only soft thing about him was his lips, and even those looked like they would bruise.

He sprawled elegantly in a chair behind the table, so perfectly still that it was eerie. I shouldn't be processing him anew, like I was seeing him for the first time, but I was.

The Grey that I knew today was an entirely different man.

But *this* man...

He was dangerous. Deadly.

God, how he'd changed. At least around me. I was

sure the rest of Guild City still knew him as this quiet, deadly predator. But I'd almost forgotten what he'd been like when we'd first met.

His dark eyebrows arched up, curiosity in his eyes. He said nothing, but he didn't need to. It was a summons. A command.

I stepped forward, my heart thundering.

He had no idea who I was. Who I was to *him*.

It would be centuries yet before I would meet him.

I drew in a steady breath and ascended the stairs to the raised platform upon which he sat.

"Madam." His voice was as cold as his eyes. "You dare much to approach my table without an introduction."

I smiled. "You've no idea what I would dare."

Interest flickered in his eyes. "Your accent. It is unusual. Foreign."

Foreign to this time, not this place. I was pure London, circa 2020. But I couldn't tell him that. So I merely inclined my head. Without asking, I took the seat across from him.

The slightest smile threatened to tug at his mouth, but he kept it suppressed. I wouldn't have noticed it if I were meeting him for the first time, but I'd grown used to his quirks.

"Well?" he asked.

I gave a slight shrug, attempting to force my face into

bored lines. "I have something I'd like to discuss with you. Privately."

His eyebrows rose again. "Really?"

"Indeed." I smiled. "It is in regard to Petra."

That time, he did nothing to disguise his naked curiosity. "How do you know of that?"

Because you told me.

Petra was a dangerous but valuable business venture from this century that Grey had remembered, an irresistible lure to the Devil that I knew next to nothing about.

"I'll discuss it in your chambers." I stood, my heartbeat thundering beneath his gaze, and prayed he couldn't hear it.

"You are nervous." His gaze dropped to my chest, but he wasn't leering. He was looking at the heart that beat so frantically. "Your heart is going wild."

Damn it.

"You'd be nervous, too, if you knew what I knew." I waved my hand, gesturing for him to follow. "Come. We will discuss it."

He stood, his chair scraping backward quietly. "How do you know that I will follow?"

I looked back at him and smiled, hoping it was mysterious. Confident. "But of course you will."

I descended the stairs, praying.

When I reached the ground below, I felt his presence

at my side. I hurried forward, trying to keep him from touching me.

I wanted him. I couldn't help it. He was Grey, in a sense.

And yet he wasn't, and it felt disloyal.

Fortunately, he was polite, though that didn't stop him from leaning down and whispering against my ear, "How do you know where my chambers are?"

I shivered at the feeling of his warm breath, heat flushing through me. "I have my ways."

I strode through the club, and the patrons parted like water to let me pass. It was so unlike when I'd had to push my way through the crowd, and I knew that I had the Devil at my back to thank for that.

We reached the exit of the club and slipped out into the quiet hall. I started down the hall, the Devil at my side.

Tension tightened the air between us.

"How do I know I can I trust you?" His voice murmured low.

"Does it matter?" I looked up at him, smiling. "You are stronger."

"Perhaps." He shrugged lightly, his gaze moving over me. It flared with heat. "But I've learned not to underestimate others. Particularly women."

We reached the door to his flat. It was time. I was going to touch him. To seduce him—at least a little. It was part of the plan.

My heart raced.

I pushed him against the door, my gaze on his lips. Heat flared, an atom bomb of attraction exploding in the space between us.

"It's wise not to underestimate me." I looked at his lips, leaning up slowly.

His hands came to my waist, gripping firmly. I shivered at the familiar touch.

Before my lips could reach his, the door behind him opened. I caught sight of *my* Grey standing behind him. He reached up with a cloth and pressed it over the other's mouth, pulling him back into the room.

Briefly, he struggled, but the potion soaking the cloth was enough to knock him out for days. He collapsed against Grey, who dragged him inside. I followed, shutting the door behind me.

The interior of the flat was quite different than I remembered. The same massive window revealed a view of a windswept desert, and the bookshelves were still there, but the furniture was older and more staid, fussier than the Grey I knew. But then, everything during this time period had been fussier.

"Where will you put him?" I asked. The potion was supposed to last for at least two days, and he'd wake with little memory of the preceding hours.

"In the second bedroom." He heaved the body into his arms and strode in that direction.

I followed him.

Grey delivered the body to the smaller bed, then stared at the younger man for a moment too long.

"Weird to see yourself like this, isn't it?" I asked.

"It is. But...that's not what's so strange." He looked down at me. "I remember this now. Waking up in this bed chamber, confused about why I was here. And realizing that two days had passed."

"What?" My heart raced. "Really?"

He nodded. "I'd forgotten it along the years, chalking it up to an excess of drink, though that was never my inclination. But now that I stand here and witness myself lying in this bed, I remember it."

"That's wild." We had proof that we were integrated into the past. "Does that mean we succeeded when we were here?"

"I do not know, unfortunately."

I nodded. We'd just have to continue forth and pray this worked. With one last look at the prone body of the former Grey, I left the room, passing Grey's usual bedroom and spotting an enormous bed draped in heavy fabric. The large window still provided a magical view of the snow-covered mountains of Carpathia, but like the rest of the flat, the decor was massively different.

I strolled over to the window, drawn by the cold, bleak landscape. It reminded me of Grey when I'd first met him.

"Do you like it?" he asked.

I looked back at him. "Parts of it, yes. It's beautiful."

"Of all the things in this flat, it most reminds me of home." He joined me, staring at the view and seeming to draw energy from it.

"It speaks to you, doesn't it?"

He nodded. "It feeds my soul, I think."

"I can see how that might be. Just like some people are rejuvenated by the seashore, this is what works for you."

"Yes. Precisely."

I smiled at him, then returned to the main living room and sat on the couch.

"Ugh." I shifted, looking up at Grey, who had followed me. "Very uncomfortable."

"That is one thing I appreciate about the present. The conveniences are far nicer." He strode to the bookshelf and inspected it. "We need a plan."

He was right. We'd come to the end of what we'd been able to map out before arrival. Now that we were here, we needed to seek the clues the book promised. So far, none of the things I'd seen had been surrounded by a faint glow of magic like Seraphia had said.

I pulled the book from my pocket and opened it, studying the page. The text was still strange and unreadable, but the memory of the woman flashed into my mind.

I looked up at Grey. "When I touched Rasla, I used my power. Tried to find a way to get the information we needed. And I saw a woman. Older, holding a mop."

"A cleaning woman?"

"I think so." I searched my memory of her. She looked nothing like Rasla, so I doubted she was family. "But a cleaning woman would know quite a lot about her boss, wouldn't she?"

"Indeed. If it was his housekeeper, she might know what we are looking for."

I closed my eyes and searched the image of her. It felt burned into my mind, and I prayed that I might recall a helpful detail. Her eyes...they were the loveliest shade of blue.

"How do we reach her?" I asked.

"I will call my second in command to come here. We can inquire. If he does not know, he can find the information."

"Do you remember who your second is?" I couldn't imagine remembering so many people over so many years.

"Honestly, I do not." Concern flickered in his eyes. "If I don't recognize him, I will just have to fake it."

12

———

I rose and walked to the door. A series of bells hung alongside the wall, and I pulled the one that corresponded to my second's station—I hoped.

A few moments later, a faint knock sounded at the door. I opened it, and a slim, middle-aged man stood there. His fair hair was swept neatly off his forehead, and his suit was immaculately pressed, the buckles on his shoes shining brilliantly.

Recognition flared.

"My lord." He bowed.

"Clarence." I stepped back, gesturing for him to enter. I waved toward Carrow. "Please meet Madam Clifton. She is visiting for a short while."

Clarence's eyes shot toward her and widened for the briefest moment.

He was surprised that a woman was here, of course. I rarely allowed women into my chambers, now or in the present.

Clarence turned toward me. "What can I do for you, my lord? Was the club not satisfactory tonight?"

"I am looking for information about a woman. The housekeeper of Councilor Raslạ, I believe. An older woman with…" I looked toward Carrow.

She filled in the details. "With brilliant blue eyes."

Clarence nodded, his own eyes brightening. "Ah, yes. Mrs. Birch-Cleve. She recently left her post, I believe."

Of course. I remembered now. Clarence had been an insatiable gossip, which had proved extremely useful for me in the past. He'd kept tabs on the goings-on in the houses of all the Council members and important people in town.

"Would you know where to find this Mrs. Birch-Cleve?" I asked.

Clarence nodded. "I'm sure I could find her quite quickly, my lord."

"Thank you." We'd need a bit more time to plan. "Could you please bring us a late meal?"

He bowed. "Of course. It will be here momentarily."

He disappeared quickly and quietly. I turned to Carrow. "That's our woman. We can visit her tomorrow morning."

Carrow nodded, frowning. "Would the Devil of Darkvale normally visit a housekeeper?"

"No, excellent point." I tapped a finger to my lips. "Perhaps it's better if she comes here. But how? She'd likely be too afraid to visit me."

"I have just the thing." Carrow reached into her pocket and withdrew a small object, holding it out to me. "This is Councilor Rasla's seal. We can send her a letter using it. She'll think she's returning to her employer."

"Excellent." I looked around my rooms. "She should not visit here. I'd hate to confuse the past version of myself if someone mentions her visit."

Carrow nodded. "What's a neutral meeting point in old Guild City?"

"The Mages' coffee shop. We can get a private room there."

"Perfect."

I stood and went to the writing desk in the corner, drawing out a piece of paper and a quill. It took a moment to become adjusted to the quill again. Damn, pens were superior. I composed a short letter to the housekeeper. When I finished, Carrow handed me the seal.

It came as second nature to find the wax and flame, creating a hot puddle on the folded parchment. I pressed the seal into it, then handed it back to Carrow. "That should do it."

A knock sounded at the door, and I went to answer it, the letter in my hand.

Clarence stood at the door, a maid at his side. Each carried a tray, and I permitted them entrance. They placed their burdens on the large table near the bookshelf, and the maid curtsied and scurried out.

Clarence looked at me. "Will that be all, my lord?"

I handed him the letter. "See that this is delivered to the housekeeper and let me know when it is done."

He nodded and took the note, then strode from the room.

I turned toward Carrow. "Now, we wait."

Her stomach grumbled faintly, and she pressed a hand to it. "Good, because I'm famished. What did you eat back then? Or...back now."

"Let's see." I strode to the table and removed the silver tops from the trays, revealing cuts of meat, vegetables, potatoes, and some form of unrecognizable pie. "Looks close enough to modern food that I think you'll be satisfied."

Carrow grinned. "I'm just glad it's not eel pie."

"There's no promising that." I pointed to the pie. "But I doubt it is eel. I've never fancied it."

"Thank God."

We ate in silence. Every moment that passed tightened the air with tension. Once we'd finished, I rose and went to the bedroom. There used to be a bathtub that would magically fill itself.

I found it in front of the fireplace, just as I'd expected. The tub was filling with water, the clear, steaming liquid rising with every second.

I turned back to the main living room and went to the door, spotting Carrow as she stood. "There's a bath here, if you like."

"Oh, that would be amazing. We haven't been here long, but I feel filthy."

I left the room, giving her privacy.

The bookshelf called to me, and I strolled to it, selecting a volume at random. As soon as I sat down on the couch to read, I heard the first splash.

Images of Carrow in the bath, her golden skin bathed by firelight, flashed in my mind.

I looked down at the brown leather book. Suddenly, it was laughable that I might be able to distract myself with seventeenth-century literature when Carrow was naked in the other room.

I tilted my head back, staring at the ceiling. How was I going to bear this?

"Grey?" Her voice filtered out from the bedroom. "Do you want to join me?"

Yes.

"The tub is very large," she said.

I drew in an unsteady breath. Most of my brain cells seemed to have perished as soon as I began thinking of Carrow in the bath. The few that had survived did their best to sort out whether it was wise to join her.

We'd been trying to avoid the thing between us, but why?

The curse had already sunk its hooks into us.

Unable to help myself, I rose and walked to the door, leaning against it so that I could see Carrow.

As I'd expected, she lounged in the bath, the water lapping at her collarbones. It was a bloody large bathtub, sufficient for at least two. I didn't recall using it with others while I'd lived here initially, but the sight of Carrow made my blood run hot.

"Join me?" she asked.

"I'm not sure it's wise." My voice sounded raspy to my own ears.

"I think we're already in trouble," she said. "If we're going to survive this, we will. If we aren't, we won't. But I think, tonight…" She shrugged, the gesture nonchalant despite the heat in her eyes. "Seems worth it."

Fates, did it ever.

"I don't want to think about the terrible things to come," she said. "And if this is all we're going to get, then I want it."

I did, too. So badly. Desire surged inside me, making me go uncomfortably hard.

And she was right. Terrible things were coming. We'd try to stop them, but we might not manage.

I didn't want to waste tonight.

I stripped off my shirt. Her gaze moved over me,

heating more with every second. My blood rushed through my veins, and my muscles tightened.

Being surrounded by evidence of my past only high-lighted how lucky I was to have her. Everything had been so dark for so long.

And now she was here. Light.

Last time we'd been together, we'd been in a dream. It had still been real, somehow. A product of her magic. But there had been a vaguely filmy quality about it.

This was clear as day, and it made it all the more intense.

I kicked off my boots and stripped out of the rest of my clothing, trembling slightly. I stepped into the bath, the water warm and welcoming. She smiled up at me, pulling me down to join her. Heat enveloped me, and she climbed onto my lap.

"Grey," she whispered, wrapping her legs around me.

I groaned, fitting her tight against me. Impossible warmth and softness. I crushed my mouth to hers, wanting to absorb every inch of her. Her scent wrapped around me, lavender and lovely. I drew my mouth from hers, running it down her damp neck.

She still tasted slightly of sweat, the faintest tang of salt. I lapped at it, my fangs growing longer at the scent of her blood beneath her skin. The beast inside me roared, wanted to bite. To drink.

I shuddered and drew back. She whimpered her disappointment.

"Too dangerous," I murmured, moving my mouth lower, to her breasts.

Her disappointment turned to pleasure as I swept my tongue over the soft skin of her chest. She clutched my head tightly, holding me to her as she moved her hips, seeking my hardness with her softness.

"Please, Grey. I don't want to wait anymore." The desperation in her voice made my heart race.

I didn't want to, either. Couldn't.

I reached between us, finding the softness there, wanting to know she was ready.

"Now." She clutched at my shoulders.

I fitted myself to her flesh, moving slowly as I sank into her. Every inch was heaven. She surrounded me— her body, her scent, her moans, her magic. I lost myself in her, wanting to live inside this moment forever.

Finally, she tightened around me, crying out against my ear. Her pleasure dragged me over the edge.

13

———

CARROW

I woke full of hope. Maybe it had been last night —*amazing*—or maybe it was the fact that we'd time traveled, thus proving that anything was possible.

But the way I figured it, if we could walk through time and visit the past, then anything could happen. And today, we were going to break the curse on Grey and me.

I wanted to wake up with him every morning that I could, and I refused to settle for the scraps that fate wanted to give me. I was going to force our life together to be what I wanted.

By the time we'd woken and dressed, we were nearly late. Grey checked on the body of his former self while I pulled on my boots and cloak. Once again, the morning looked dreary, as if the entire seventeenth century were miserable.

Grey returned from the second bedroom, looking handsome as ever, even in his strange old clothing. It was a style that had always appeared a bit funny in old paintings, but on him, it looked good.

"He's fine," Grey said. "Let's go. We don't want to be late."

I finished fastening my cloak. "How's the coffee in this century?"

"Not what you're used to."

"No frappes?" I teased.

"Certainly not. Though the pastries are not terrible."

At the thought of them, my stomach growled. We'd both worked up an appetite last night.

Together, we left his flat, making our way quickly through the magic-lit hallways. When we reached the front foyer where Miranda usually stood, I was almost surprised not to see her there.

Instead, it was Clarence. Grey stopped by briefly. "No cleaning today, Clarence. My rooms are to remain undisturbed."

"Very good, my lord." Clarence nodded. "You've a meeting with Madam Stockhausen this evening."

Grey frowned, and I could tell that he was trying to remember what it was about. Finally, he said, "Please reschedule until the day after tomorrow."

Clarence nodded. "Of course. And one more thing. Councilor Rasla came by to ask for you. And about your guest."

My soul chilled at the thought.

"We have no business with him," Grey said. "Turn him away next time."

"I will do so. Have a fine day, my lord."

"You as well, Clarence." Grey turned, and I followed him out into the drizzly morning. "I suppose that answers the question of whether he recognized me."

"Yeah. Not good." The air was cool and wet, a welcome refresher until I had my caffeine. I sucked in a breath, trying to drive away the thought of Rasla. "Any idea who Madam Stockhausen is?"

"Not a clue. But hopefully, we'll be done by then, and my previous self will be conscious." He shook his head. "And I'll have to determine how Rasla resisted my magic so that I can erase his memory of us."

We made our way across town, headed for the Mages' coffee shop. The morning crowd was out and about, but everything still looked so different compared to the Guild City that I knew. True, the bones were there—the roads and buildings were the same, but they looked newer. The people, however, looked older, more worn down. Even supernaturals were subject to the difficulties of life in the past. Everything was louder, dirtier, busier.

Finally, we reached the square in front of the Mages'

Guild. I spotted their enormous coffee shop and whistled low. "It looks fab."

Grey nodded, his gaze moving over the façade. It looked much nicer than the building I remembered. The plaster gleamed white between the straight, dark wooden beams. The windows glittered, even though the sun was well hidden, and the structure looked like it was standing up a bit straighter. That could be said of the whole town, in fact. Time hadn't yet worn on the buildings, and it showed.

"It's brand new," Grey said. "Come." He strode across the square, and I followed.

Noise filtered through the windows as we neared, the sound of boisterous conversation and laughter. Grey opened the door, and I entered, inspecting every inch of the coffee shop that I could see.

Like the outside, everything looked nicer and straighter than the place I'd visited in my time. The ceiling wasn't quite as slanted, and everything gleamed with the shine of newness.

The bar was in the same location and the same size, though the massive, whirring espresso machines were nowhere to be seen. There were other coffee-making apparatuses, though—gleaming metal and glass containers that billowed steam.

It was far warmer inside, and I reached up to remove my cloak.

A host stood near the door, his clothing impeccable. He spotted Grey and approached.

"My lord." His voice echoed with reverence, reminding me that my mate was the most powerful person in Guild City.

Grey inclined his head. "A private room, please. We have someone meeting us soon. An older woman named Mrs. Birch-Cleve."

"But of course." The man's eyes gleamed with excitement. "Follow me."

He hurried off toward the stairs, and we followed. As I crossed the coffee shop, I peeked into the various rooms that I could see. As before, there was one dedicated to music—albeit far older music than I preferred. Another room was full of people playing games, and yet another dedicated to quiet reading. Students, maybe. They all looked young. I would have loved to come back here and explore more in this time, but I had a feeling that Seraphia would say it was too dangerous. Since I risked being stuck here, I couldn't help but agree.

The host led us to a quiet room with a large window overlooking the street. The dark floor was level and smooth, unlike the floors of this place in the present day, and the fireplace flickered with a warm light.

"Please, sit." The host gestured to the table in front of the window. "I will show your guest up when she arrives."

"Thank you." Grey sat, and I joined him.

"Do we order the same way that we do in the present?" I asked.

He nodded. "They implemented the spell when they first opened, and that hasn't changed."

Grey waved his hand across the middle of the table, and golden light swirled over the dark wood. Images of various coffees appeared, floating in midair. They were different than the cappuccinos and lattes I'd seen the first time I visited. Instead, there were black coffees of various sizes, tea, and something that looked like hot chocolate.

I chose a black coffee, and Grey did the same.

"Now for breakfast." He waved his hand over the table again, and a variety of tarts appeared, most of them unrecognizable.

I frowned at them. "Could you choose something savory and not weird for me?"

"No eel pie?"

"Not at this hour." *Not at any hour.*

Grey chose two pastries that looked like they might contain egg and ham. "I think you'll like this. Or tolerate it."

I smiled. Our drinks and food appeared a moment later, and I drank quickly, ignoring the heat. As soon as our guest showed up, I'd likely be too busy to drink my coffee, and I didn't want to start this day without caffeine.

A few moments later, the woman from my vision

arrived. Her beige dress was threadbare, and she looked tired. When her gaze landed on us, she stutter-stepped, her blue eyes flashing.

"You are not Councilor Rasla." Her accent was a bit old fashioned, like Rasla's had been, but I could understand her.

"We aren't." I stood. "But please, don't leave. We need your help."

Her gaze moved over us warily. She stared at Grey for a particularly long time. "What does the Devil of Darkvale want with the likes of me?"

"Your help," he said, his voice soft.

Her face crumpled in a frown. "My help?"

"Please, sit." He gestured. "Order anything you like."

"All right." She approached cautiously, taking the seat closer to me.

I sat next to her while she ordered. Once she had food and drink in front of her, she looked up at us. "You'd best explain. I wouldn't have come if the letter hadn't contained Rasla's seal. How did you get it?"

Did I explain that I'd found it more than three hundred years into the future? No. Instead, I just said, "We stole it."

Her eyebrows rose. "You dared?" She scoffed. "Of course you dared. You're the Devil of Darkvale," she muttered at Grey.

"Why did you think that Rasla was asking you to meet here?" he asked.

"Honestly, I did not know." She shrugged. "But I feared repercussions if I did not come, so here I am."

"Something went wrong at Councilor Rasla's house, and you left your post, is that correct?" Grey asked, concern in his voice.

She nodded, her expression haunted. "I could stay there no longer. And yes, leaving led to hard times. Won't be able to keep my home, come winter. The money will run out."

Grey reached into his pocket and withdrew a pouch that jingled with coins. "Whatever forced you to leave is unfair and unfortunate." He set the pouch on the table in front of it. "That is for you."

She frowned and took it, looking inside. Her brows rose, and her face went white. "This would see me until the end of my days." Suspicion flashed in her eyes. "Why? What do you want in exchange?"

"That is yours to keep no matter what happens here," he said. "I dislike unfairness, and while I do not understand the details of your situation, I have no doubt that Councilor Rasla is to blame. A housekeeper would not leave her post without promise of a referral."

"That is true enough." She shrugged as if that were obvious. "But still, you must want something from me."

"Information, if you are willing to give it," Grey said. "If you are not, then I would use my power to compel you to tell me. It would not hurt you, but I would leave with the information I need. Either way, the money is yours."

She scoffed again, which seemed to be her signature expression. "You're honest, I'll give you that."

"As I said, I would see to it that no harm comes to you," Grey said. "But it is a matter of life and death. Of *my* life and death, and that of the woman I care for."

Her eyes darted to me, considering. "I do not recognize you."

"I'm not a resident of Guild City," I replied. "Not *this* Guild City, at least.

"So you've given me this money to ease my way." She hefted the pouch. "And you'll have the information you want, whether or not I give it to you of my own volition."

"That is essentially it, yes," Grey said.

"You could have just taken the information." She frowned at him. "That's the reputation associated with you."

"I suppose so." Grey shrugged. "Perhaps I am a changed man."

Her eyes moved to me again. "Love."

He said nothing, but I couldn't help but look at him. Just briefly. Then I turned to the woman. "Will you help us?"

"Yes. And you'd best be grateful, because your power would not work on my mind. It is too strong." Pride echoed in her voice.

"Really?" Grey leaned forward, interest in his eyes.

"Indeed. Part of my magic." She gestured to herself. "Try."

Grey's brows rose, and then he spoke, his voice echoing with his power. "Tell me the date of your birth."

She smiled. "No."

"Tell me a secret from your childhood. Something harmless."

"No." She shook her head.

Grey stared at her a moment. "That's quite impressive."

"Indeed. Like I said, my mind is quite powerful."

"What species are you?" I asked.

"Witch. From a long line. My mother was the same." She looked at Grey. "So I suppose it is good that you showed me kindness and honesty. I will help you."

"Thank you," Grey said.

My gaze moved to the money he'd given her. It had been a thoughtful gesture. Would the Devil have done that in this time? Somehow, I thought not. Even the Devil I'd known when I'd first come to Guild City would not have thought of it.

But Grey had. He was changing.

I liked it.

The woman leaned forward. "What do you want to know?"

This was the tricky part. We were looking for information about me. About my powers and my past. And somehow, Rasla was tied up in all of this. The woman

I'd seen in my vision was tied up in this. But where did we start?

"Are you familiar with the Shadow Guild?" Grey asked.

It was as good a place as any to start.

Fear flashed in her eyes, turning the blue dark. "How do you know of that? I thought I was the only one who knew, besides Councilor Rasla."

"Really?" I leaned forward. "What do you mean?"

She swallowed hard and lowered her voice. "The Shadow Guild was real. I swear on my eternal soul. The tower was on the far side of town, near the gate through the Haunted Hound. But it's gone now because of Councilor Rasla."

"He erased the town's memories of it," I said. "Did he not erase yours?"

"Oh, he tried, but the magic did not work on me. My mind is too strong, as I said. But he erased it in the memories of everyone else in town. Even in the memories of those who had once been in the guild. For a while, I spoke of it, trying to find someone else who remembered. But no one did."

"And then what?" I asked.

"Eventually, I drew too much attention from Councilor Rasla. He'd worked so hard to hide what he'd done. If he learned that I knew..." She shook her head, and it was clear she feared for her life. "I left my post, hoping to find other work and that he would forget me."

"What happened to the members of the Shadow Guild?" Grey asked.

It was a good question. The council evicted anyone who didn't have a guild. Where were they? Still in Guild City?

"Most of them are outcasts now. Nearly all have left town," she said. "He didn't even care that his own daughter was in the guild."

"His daughter?" Excitement thrummed in my chest.

"Yes." Mrs. Birch-Cleve nodded. "His daughter, Evangeline Rasla. His only child."

"Why does he hate the Shadow Guild so much?" I asked. "And his own daughter?"

Her eyes shifted left and right. "I'll confess, I found this information in the tried and true way of all house-keepers. I snooped."

All right then. Fantastic.

"Rasla should have been in the Shadow Guild," she continued. "His father was the guild leader, you see, and the Rasla family comes from a long line of those with strange magic. But Councilor Rasla himself—full mage. Nothing unique about him, besides his particular talent for manipulating people's minds. But he's not so talented that he could lead, and he couldn't bear it. Neither a member of the Shadow Guild, nor a leader of his own."

"And that was enough to make him destroy the Shadow Guild?" I asked.

She shook her head. "Not just that. His father was a hard man. Demanding. Not cruel, not quite. But Councilor Rasla had a terrible relationship with him, ever since the moment he could talk. Those two were ever at odds, I tell you. The fights would do my head in. Vicious, so vicious that they seemed like animals."

"Which one was in the wrong?" I asked. Was Rasla an abused boy or a bastard?

"Both, if you ask me. Neither man was evil. But combined, they brought out the worst in each other. And when Rasla learned he would never be in the Shadow Guild and that his power was a fraction of his father's? Well..." She shook her head.

"So Rasla destroyed the Shadow Guild as revenge against his father?" I asked.

She nodded. "Once he joined the Mages' Guild, he began to work against his father. In small things at first, gradually growing larger. It went on for decades, until finally, his granddaughter was born. That was too much for him."

"Granddaughter?" Was she the woman I'd seen in my vision? No, Rasla was too young to have a grown granddaughter.

She nodded. "His only daughter had a daughter of her own. When she was born, her magic was unlike anything anyone had ever seen. She can touch a person's soul. Pull it right out of their body, if she wishes."

"How old is she?" Grey asked.

"Not more than a year, I'd say."

"She can do this as a *baby*?" I asked. "Before she even knows what she's doing?"

"Yes. She's never harmed anyone. It is more like…an act of love, I suppose. She fills you with such joy that your soul tries to leave your body to be with her." She shuddered. "It is an odd feeling—good and bad at the same time. I've felt it but once."

"How did you survive?"

"It wasn't a forcible thing," she said. "I could feel my soul moving toward her, and I pulled it back into myself."

"But that magic must be incredible." I looked at Grey for confirmation that this was strange.

He nodded.

"It is," the woman said. "And that baby would lead the Shadow Guild one day, no doubt. He couldn't bear such a constant reminder of his failure. A short while later, the tower disappeared, and everyone in town acted like it was the most normal thing in the world. He used magic unlike any I'd ever seen, combined with his gift for controlling people's minds."

What a bastard.

The woman leaned toward me. "You look quite a lot like her, you know. Rasla's daughter. The spitting image."

I'd looked a bit like the woman in my vision. Though

I hadn't been able to see her clearly, the similarities had been there.

She had to have been Rasla's daughter. Which meant we were related. The seer had said to seek my past, and she'd been right.

14

I watched Carrow's face pale as she stared at the old woman.

"I really look like Rasla's daughter?" she asked.

"Almost exactly the same. Like you could be related. Not that anyone in town would recognize you. He's made people forget his daughter's face, I believe. Forget that she ever existed." Mrs. Birch-Cleve shook her head in disgust, then peered at me. "There's quite a bit more to you, too, I imagine."

"What does that mean?" she asked.

The woman smiled enigmatically. "I've told you all I know."

I believed her, just as I believed that Carrow was

related to Rasla. Not only because she looked like the daughter, but because it was the missing piece we'd been looking for—Carrow's past.

She'd found the Shadow Guild on her own. Saved the place and been chosen the leader, though she seemed hesitant to take on the mantle. It had been foretold by fate, and the pieces were coming together.

"Where would we find the daughter?" I asked the woman.

"The last I knew, she was still in Rasla's house. Locked away." She shook her head. "Though I fear for her."

I nodded. "Thank you for all that you have done."

Carrow stared at the woman, questions in her eyes.

The woman reached for her hand, squeezing it. "I've told you all that I know, dearie. In God's name, I swear it."

Carrow nodded. "Do you mind if I try my magic on you? I can read things from people and objects. A bit like a seer."

"You're no seer, dearie." The woman nodded. "But you may try your power on me. I will not stop you."

Carrow nodded and closed her eyes, her magic flaring. The scent of lavender filled the air, and I inhaled deeply. I loved her scent—would breathe it in every minute of every day if I could.

A few minutes later, Carrow withdrew her hand. "Thank you."

"No, thank *you*. This will make a great difference to me." The woman lifted the bag of money I'd left. It was the least I could to.

But I should warn her. I leaned toward her. "The Devil of Darkvale that you know—I am not that man. If you were to approach him, he would not recognize you."

Her blue eyes searched my face, and she nodded. "Yes. You do seem quite different. No layer of ice about you, as there usually is."

"Hardly," I said.

She smiled. "Well, perhaps the ice is thinner, then. But don't you worry. I've enough now to see me through nicely. I won't go getting myself into trouble with the other version of you."

I nodded and set another coin on the table to pay for our meal.

Carrow and I left, moving quickly down the stairs and out of the coffee shop. As we crossed the courtyard, she leaned close. "I'm related to Rasla. I'm sure of it now."

"As am I." I looked down at her. "Is that what you saw when you used your power?"

She nodded. "I saw the daughter again, and that woman is right. We're so alike."

"Let's go find her. I know where Rasla lives." I led us through town, which had become busier since morning. We headed toward Black Church and the neighborhood where Councilor Rasla owned a home. It was one of the larger ones in town, on one of the better streets.

As we turned down the road, I inspected each building. As expected, the doors were shut tight, and there were quite a few people milling about.

"We won't want to enter via the front," I said. "There's no way to stay unseen. But each of these homes contains a walled garden at the back, accessed via an alley."

"Lead the way," Carrow said.

I cut through the crowd, pulling my hat down low so that people didn't notice me. Fortunately, most people on this street were too busy going about their business to pay attention. We reached a quieter side street and cut down the cobblestone lane, reaching the darkened alley at the back. On either side of us, stone walls rose three meters tall, concealing the gardens on either side.

"Why do they have these alleys back here? They're awful," Carrow said.

I had to agree. It smelled faintly of sewage, and I pointed to the drains that led to the sewer system below the city. "This is how Guild City dealt with waste. Magic can handle a small amount of it, but a city this size needs the help of engineering that hasn't been invented yet. So this is the solution. The maids in each house will come back here to dispose of household refuse."

"That's quite impressive, considering it's 1642."

"It's far more advanced than the system in human

London, and magic is used to keep it flowing at a reasonable rate and stench. Still, it's disgusting."

As if to highlight my point, a few rats darted out of the sewer.

"How do you know which garden is his?" Carrow asked.

"If I remember Rasla at all, it will be fairly ostentatious." I inspected each of the heavy wooden doors as I passed. Finally, I spotted one with a brass crest and pointed to it. "That's it."

Carrow looked at it. "It's just like his seal."

I nodded, hovering my hand over the door. Magic pricked against my palm. "There's a charm. Moderate strength."

"I'm sure I've got something for that." She reached into the bag at her side, rummaging around until she found what she was looking for. A moment later, she held up a glowing blue vial of potion. "This should break the charm."

She worked quickly, uncorking the vial and pouring the liquid on the iron door handle. Magic sparked and popped, then faded. With a grin, she pushed open the door.

I gripped her shoulder gently to stall her and slipped through first, watching warily for attack. The garden was unremarkable, rectangular and surrounded on all sides by walls. Neatly laid out paths and benches and hedges created a space to enjoy the outdoors, but no one was there.

Magic still sparked on the air, however, and I doubted we were in the clear. I turned back to Carrow. "It's safe presently, but we're probably not past the worst of it."

She nodded and followed me in. A path cut down the center of the garden, leading directly to the back of the tall, narrow house.

Together, we approached the house, our senses alert. We'd just crossed the midway point when a vine shot out from the wall and wrapped around my leg. I stumbled, nearly going to my knees. Another vine lashed out, wrapping around my arm. They burned, some type of magic that made my skin feel as if it were on fire.

I drew a blade from the ether and severed the vine at my arm, then the one at my leg.

Beside me, a thick vine wrapped around Carrow's waist. She hissed with pain and called on her own blade. I swung around to cut the vine from her, but two more wrapped around my arm before I could.

I thrashed, my muscles burning, and broke through the vines. Two more wrapped around my legs, and I sliced them off. Carrow cut the one around her waist, but two more grabbed her. They were so damned fast that she didn't stand a chance. I could barely keep up, and only because of my enhanced speed.

More and more vines lashed out from the walls, and

I sliced at them as quickly as I could, taking them out one by one. There were too many, though. Three wrapped around me, and Carrow was covered in far more.

She sagged to the ground, her eyes closing. Fear pierced me. "Hang on, Carrow!"

My heart thundered with fear as I fought the vines, desperate to get to her. I was fast enough to keep them off myself, but not fast enough to reach her. More and more vines wrapped around her, so many that she was disappearing.

Her magic filled the air, the scent of lavender strong.

She was using her power.

Her eyes snapped open and met mine. "Kill the base of the plant by the wall."

Hope flared, and I hacked at the vines that trapped my legs, the pain of their burn making my skin chill. I couldn't imagine what Carrow felt with so many vines around her. Fear for her drove me, making me quicker and stronger. I fought off the vines and sprinted toward the wall, seeking the base of the plant.

It grew from the edge of the garden, and I lunged for it, slicing at the base, hacking at the thick growth with all of my strength.

Finally, I cut through the last of it. The vines withered, turning thin and brown. I raced back to Carrow, finding her limp against the ground, the vines dying around her.

I yanked them off, my heart pounding.

"Carrow." Fear echoed in my voice as I shook her gently. "Wake up. You're fine. You're fine."

"That felt like hell," she rasped, her eyes opening.

I hugged her to me gently, running kisses over her brow. "That was quick thinking."

"Well, I wasn't having any luck with my knife." She pulled back from me slightly, the color returning to her cheeks. "As much as I'd like to continue this, we need to get moving."

"Do you feel all right?"

She nodded, rising slowly to her feet and shaking out her skirts. "The pain has mostly faded. Once the vines died, it started to go."

I inspected her for any wounds but saw none. "Ready?"

"Lead on."

We headed down the path, our guard up and our movements silent. Finally, we reached the back of the house, an impressive three-story structure covered with rose vines. There were two doors to choose from, and I went for the smaller one that looked like the servants' entrance.

The door opened silently, and I entered a dimly lit kitchen that made me grateful for the twenty-first century. The drab room was lit by a large fire, the heat oppressive. The scent of cured meat permeated the place.

A woman in a simple dress, who'd been stoking the fire, turned as I entered. Her eyes widened, and her hand flew to her chest. "Who are you?"

"Calm yourself, madam, and sit in that chair." I imbued my voice with my power and pointed to the small wooden chair by the fire.

Her eyes went foggy, thank fates, and she drifted over to the chair.

At my side, Carrow whispered. "Is this really the kitchen?"

"Archaic, I know." I strode to the woman, crouching down in front of her. "Is Councilor Rasla's daughter here?"

"Who?" Confusion flickered in her voice. "He has no daughter."

"Tell me the truth," I commanded, making sure that her eyes blurred and that my power was working on her.

"It is the truth, my lord. Just him. Always has been."

I shared a look with Carrow. Between the housekeeper and this maid, I knew who I believed. Rasla's magic had worked on her, it seemed, and her memories were gone.

"Is there anyone else in the house?" I asked. "Another maid, perhaps?"

"No one. Not now."

That would make things easier. "Stay here for an hour, then return to your duties. Forget you ever saw us."

She nodded slowly, settling back against the chair to wait. I stood. Carrow was already moving toward the door, heading into the rest of the house. I followed, loathing the cramped, dark interior. Even the nicest, largest houses in this period had low ceilings and heavy architecture. My tower wasn't much different, but it had been modified to suit me and the changing times.

We entered a sitting room at the front of the house. Glittering mullioned windows provided a partial view of the street outside, but not enough light to brighten the dark wood and thick fabrics that covered the furniture. The fireplace lay cold and silent.

Carrow walked around the room, running her hands over the furniture and paintings, the lavender scent of her magic trailing behind her.

"I'm not getting much," she said. "Mostly images of Rasla."

She closed her eyes, her magic flaring brighter. I tasted oranges and salt, a lovely combination. Her face flushed as she tried harder to access the information she wanted.

Finally, she opened her eyes. "The daughter was here, but rarely came into this room. Let's check upstairs."

We passed through another small reception room and a dining room. Carrow ignored them, heading straight for the stairs. Though there were several bedrooms on the next floor—all of them as dark and dreary as the living room—none seemed like our target. One most definitely belonged to Rasla, from the look of the large bed and filled wardrobe.

"Next floor," Carrow said.

We ascended the narrow, creaking stairs. Most of the rooms on this floor were empty. It wasn't until we came to a locked door that Carrow grinned widely. "This is it. I'm sure of it."

I knelt beside her at the door, inspecting the lock. It was an ancient thing, cast iron and heavy. Magic sparked around it, violent and sharp. "We'd be best off finding the key."

Carrow tried to touch the lock, and a bright white spark popped. She yanked her hand back, shaking it. "Yep. Let's find it."

"We should try Rasla's bedroom."

"Agreed. He seems like just the kind of control freak to keep it there."

We headed back downstairs and began to hunt through the room, searching every nook and cranny that we could find. There was nothing even remotely interesting in it, from what I could see. Rasla was a miserably dull bastard in his home life. Or perhaps he was just good at hiding.

My money was on dull.

Carrow pushed a large chair aside and stood, walking across the area where the chair had been. She stopped dead in her tracks.

I frowned. "What is it?"

She shifted her weight, her head tilted to the side. Her skirts rustled. A creaking sounded from beneath her foot, and she smiled. "Just like at Seraphia's library."

"What do you mean?"

She knelt to inspect the board that had creaked underfoot, eventually prying it up with her fingers. She reached in and pulled out a key, then grinned at me. "Just like the box Seraphia kept under the table."

"Clever."

Carrow stood and we returned to the room at the top of the stairs. The key slipped easily into the lock, twisting right. It popped open, and Carrow pulled on the door.

15

———

The room within was simple and quite sad. A narrow bed against one small window, a desk, and a crib. Drab brown walls and bedding.

"Oh, this is terrible." My gaze went to the window, where I spotted iron bars in front of the mullioned glass. "Oh, hell. Rasla is a bastard."

"What happened to her, though?" Grey walked slowly into the room. "This room has been empty for a while."

I followed him in, my skin going cold.

Please be alive.

A noise sounded from down below. A shout from the street, like a greeting. I strode to the window and looked down through the bars. We were at the front of the house, and I could see right into the street. Rasla stood beneath us, talking to a man on the other side of the road.

The sun was setting and casting shadows on the street, so it was impossible to see who he was talking to, but it didn't matter. We had only minutes left.

"He's here," I said. "He'll be coming in soon."

"He may sense something is wrong when he sees the maid sitting." Grey turned and went to the bed, beginning to search under the mattress.

My heart raced as I hurried to the desk. There was a small stack of parchment and a pen. I touched each, letting my magic flow through me. The parchment gave me no clues, but the pen lit something up inside me.

"She used this to write the book that brought us here," I said.

"Then we're definitely on the right track." Grey ducked to look under the bed, pressing on the floorboards. "There's nothing around the bed that tells where she went."

I hurried to the small cradle, searching under the little mattress. I found nothing, and sadness blasted through me as I searched. There was something so tragic and forlorn about this crib.

What had happened to them?

We could demand answers from Rasla, but he was already suspicious. Grey could use his powers to wipe his mind, but that wasn't always foolproof. It'd be better if we could find answers without running into him.

Below, I heard the door slam.

"He's inside." I rifled quickly through the blanket on the crib, my heart racing. "Hurry."

Grey paced the room, testing the floorboards with his feet. I rose to join him, then stopped.

The cradle drew my attention back to it. There were answers there. I just needed to try harder with my magic.

I knelt by the crib and gripped the wooden edge, calling upon my power.

Where are you?

Magic flared to life inside my chest, bright and strong, yet still weaker than it could be. *Come on.* I needed to try harder.

I envisioned the woman I'd seen when I'd touched the book. Imagined her now, running with her baby. Or dead.

The thought made a shudder run through me. I was afraid of what I might find, but still, I needed to find it.

Where are you?

Shouts sounded from down below.

"He's yelling at the maid," Grey said. "He'll grow suspicious soon. Hurry."

I squeezed my eyes shut and kept trying. *Come on, come on, come on.*

I could find her. I had to find her.

Finally, an image flared to life. I'd recognize the place anywhere.

I surged upright. "I've got it. The Haunted Hound. Let's get out of here."

Footsteps sounded on the stairs below, and my skin chilled. "He's coming."

"Best if we don't meet him." Grey moved swiftly and silently to the exit and took a left into the room next door. "There's a larger window here. No bars."

I followed him in, the sound of Rasla's footsteps making my breath grow short in my lungs. Grey stood near a mullioned glass window in a room filled with old furniture. It was storage space, obviously. The window wasn't the sort that opened, so Grey picked up an old chair and smashed it through the glass.

He tossed the chair aside and threw an old blanket over the jagged glass, then turned to me, holding out his hands. "Come on."

"I know it's you, Devil!" Rasla's voice sounded from below.

"Do we stay and erase his memory now, or go get our answers from Evangeline?" I asked.

"We go. There's no time to waste trying to learn how he resisted my power before. And if she's running, we can't let her get farther. We'll deal with him later."

I nodded and raced to Grey, then scrambled out the window and onto the steep roof. Grey slipped out behind me and darted gracefully to the side, moving quickly on the tiles. I followed, moving as quickly as I dared in my long dress and unfamiliar shoes, and we raced across the slanted rooftop.

"I'll find you!" Rasla's voice echoed after us.

I looked back and spotted him hanging out the broken window. It was growing dark, but there was still enough light to see the rage in his eyes.

He was totally onto us, though he probably still had no idea who I was. It would prove problematic for Grey, however. We'd need to sort this out before we returned to our time.

I followed Grey along the rooftops, climbing from building to building, and nearly losing my footing several times. We were three stories up, and a fall would be catastrophic.

"Come, we can get down right here." Grey stopped at the edge of the row of buildings where it terminated against a side street.

I stopped next to him, looking down. A sturdy vine had grown along the side of the wall, so old and tough that we could use it like a ladder.

I dropped low and scrambled over the edge. Shouts sounded from down the road to my right.

It had to be Rasla, coming our way down the street. Grey climbed alongside me, just as fast, and we reached the bottom seconds later.

"This way." Grey sprinted away from the noise, and I followed. We hurried into the dark, losing ourselves amongst the winding streets of Guild City, until the shouts of Rasla and whoever he'd gathered on his side disappeared.

Finally safe, I leaned against a wall in an old, smelly alley. Panting, I turned to Grey. "That was too close."

He nodded. "I'm going to have to find him and erase his memory, or he'll cause problems for me in this timeline."

"We'll make it a priority." I looked down the street, trying to get my bearings. "We need to go to the Haunted Hound. I think we're close.'

"We are. This way." He started down the alley, and I followed.

The streets were quiet, probably because people were home for dinner. It only took us a few minutes to reach the gate that would lead to the pub.

As we approached the gate, we kept our heads down. My shoulders relaxed when we disappeared into the darkness of the tunnel that would lead us to the Haunted Hound. We reached the portal, and the ether sucked us in, spinning us around and spitting us out in the back hallway at the pub.

I got my bearings and said, "Well, that was the most familiar thing we've done in a while."

Grey cracked a slight smile. "You'll like the Hound, then."

We walked out of the dark hallway and into the main

part of the pub. Happiness filled me at the sight. It was exactly the same as it was in the modern day. Same dark walls, low ceiling, small wooden tables, and fireplace.

"You're right," I said. "I'm still a fan."

"Ready to get back to our time?" he asked.

"More ready every second." I searched the Hound for any sight of the woman we sought.

Though there were quite a few people there, none of them were Evangeline. There were two living dogs by the fire, however, and I gasped.

"The ghost dogs are alive," I whispered.

Grey nodded. "It's called The Hound at this point, I believe. But when the dogs pass, they'll stay on, and the bar's name will change."

I loved the idea of it.

But there was no time to dawdle. I looked toward the bar, unable to help the slight disappointment at the sight of the unfamiliar person there. It was silly. Of course Mac and Quinn weren't working, no matter how similar the place looked. I was just longing for something certain and familiar.

Quickly, I strode to the bar, giving all the patrons one last look. They wore the usual attire of the period, which was the only thing different about the Hound, and I still didn't recognize anyone.

I could feel the bartender's gaze on me as we approached, and I stopped in front of him and smiled.

He was a burly man with a beard and beady eyes—nowhere near as charming or handsome as Quinn.

He gripped the rag in his hand and asked. "What can I get you?"

"I'm looking for a woman," I said.

"Don't snitch on my customers, I don't." His eyes flashed.

Grey joined me, catching the man's gaze. His voice vibrated with power as he spoke. "You will help us find the woman we seek."

The man grimaced briefly, but his eyes fogged with the power of Grey's gift. He nodded jerkily.

"She looks like me," I said. "And she should be here."

The man hissed out a breath, then spoke. "Aye, you look familiar. And there was a lady here. Stayed three nights in the room upstairs, along with her babe."

Was? "Where is she now?"

"Left only ten minutes ago," he said. "Said she was making a new life for herself in the country."

In the country was a massive place. Pretty much everything except London.

"Where?" I asked.

"Dunno. But logic says she'd be trying to get a ride with Old Robert and his carriage service."

I looked between him and Grey. "Where does that depart from?"

Grey's brow furrowed slightly as he tried to remember, and the bartender beat him to it. "From the main market in Covent Garden."

I turned to Grey. It wouldn't be the market I knew—that had been built after 1642. "Do you know where that is?"

"I should, yes." He looked at the man. "You'll forget you saw us or helped us."

The man nodded, his shoulders relaxing as if he were pleased to be rid of us. I whirled around and headed for the door, pushing my way out into London.

The stench was the first thing to hit me, making my eyes water. "Holy hell, this is terrible."

"Human London."

The smell came from all around—sewage, slop, horses. The animals clomped their way through the street, their carriage wheels rattling over the cobblestones. People pushed their way along with the crowd, and we joined the crush.

Hitching up my skirt, I ran full out, my lungs burning and elbows flying as I shoved my way through the crowd. Grey stuck close to my side, leading the way as we raced toward the main market.

"We're nearly there," he said after a few minutes.

Panting, I prayed we weren't too late. I could track her, but if we lost her in London, it might take far too much time.

"That's it, up ahead." Grey pointed to a collection of

buildings and stalls arranged around a square. Dozens of carriages sat out front, their horses tied off to posts.

I searched the space, desperate to find Evangeline. As if fate had heard my prayers, my gaze landed on a woman. I could only see her simple dress and the back of her head, but it was her. A golden light glowed around her, glittering and bright.

Just like Seraphia had said.

No one else could see it, or they'd be staring at her. But I could. Because the book was leading me to her. She was the one I was meant to find.

Evangeline.

I ran toward her, cutting through the crowd. I was nearly to her when I shouted, "Evangeline!"

She stiffened but didn't turn.

I ran to her, darting around to stand in front of her. She did look just like me. It was eerie. Same golden hair, eyes, bone structure. The baby in her arms slept silently.

Her brow furrowed as her face searched mine. "Who are you?"

"Carrow Burton." The name would mean nothing to her.

"Why do you look like me?"

"Long story." My mind raced. Where did I start?

Grey came to stand beside me, and her eyes darted to him, widening. "I know you."

Grey bowed slightly. "We haven't been formally introduced, but I am Grey."

He didn't use his title, which was rare. I'd never heard him referred to as anything other than the Devil of Darkvale, and he certainly had never asked my friends to call him Grey.

But technically, this woman was my family. It was the only logical reason we looked alike.

"What do you want with me?" The woman's eyes glanced warily to the carriages. She clearly wanted to make a run for it. Had her father erased her memory, too? What did she know?

Anything?

I pulled the book out of my pocket and showed her. "Do you recognize this?"

She looked at it blankly for the briefest moment, then recognition flared, and she gasped. She raised a hand to her head, wincing, and managed to keep a grip on her baby with her other arm. Her eyes met mine. "How did you get that?"

"I found it when I found the Shadow Guild tower hidden in Guild City. More than three hundred years from now."

She began to pant, her breath coming more quickly. She was panicking.

I reached for her arm, trying to steady her, but she stepped back. Concern shot through me. "Are you all right?"

"I will be." She forced her breathing to calm. "May I touch the book?"

"Sure." I held it out to her, confused as hell. What was going on with her?

She raised her hand to her lips and pulled her glove off with her teeth, then reached for the book and pressed her fingertips to it. She flinched, her eyes going wide and blurry. Tears began to roll down her cheeks, and she swallowed hard, forcing them to stop. After a few moments, her gaze met mine. "We should speak."

I looked at Grey. "Is there somewhere private around here?"

He looked around, his height allowing him to see over the crowd. "I believe I see a small garden over there."

"Is that okay with you?" I asked her.

"Okay?" she asked bemusedly.

"Is it good?" I corrected, remembering that she didn't understand modern slang.

She nodded, her lips pressed flat into a line.

Grey led us through the crowd, which parted easily for him. The garden was indeed relatively private, tucked back behind a locked iron gate covered in vines. Grey reached for it and yanked, breaking the lock.

"Well, that was easy," I said.

"No magic protecting it." He shook his head. "Humans."

We walked into the small garden, and he shut the gate behind us. It was about five meters by ten, vines covering most of the iron fence and gate that separated it from the bustle of dreary, gray London. Inside, the lush plants and flowers dampened the noise, making it feel like a peaceful retreat. A small, square pond sat in the middle with benches all around. I pointed to one. "Will that do for you?"

She nodded and walked toward it, clutching her baby close. Questions raced through my mind as I followed her. She had no luggage. Was this all she owned? Did she have money? Why was she leaving?

To get away from Rasla, I had to assume. I'd seen the bars on her awful room. But she was running with nothing, it seemed.

She sat on the far edge of the bench, and I joined her, leaving a small spot for Grey at the end. Silence stretched between us for a few long moments, until her gaze met mine.

"We must be family," she said, her voice questioning. "Three hundred years into the future?"

I nodded. "The year 2020."

"Oh, my." Her eyes widened. "It took you so long to find my book?"

"You left it on purpose?" I asked.

She nodded. "May I hold it again? It helps me remember what has been stolen from me."

"Remember?" I handed her the book, feeling Grey come to sit at my side. He stayed silent, tucking himself back, likely so that Evangeline could focus on me. "You mean your memories were taken like everyone else's?"

She nodded, a bitter laugh escaping her as she pressed her hand flat to the book, cradling her sleeping baby in her other arm. "My father did not spare me, of course."

"So you remember what he did? Hiding the Shadow Guild and erasing everyone's memories of it?"

"Oh, yes." She nodded her head. "I believe that only I and the housekeeper, Mrs. Birch-Cleve, know the truth. For different reasons, of course."

"Why were you running?"

"It is all quite a story." She looked down at the book. "But I believe we should start with this."

16

———

CARROW

Evangeline rubbed the book with her fingers. "It is not a simple book, as I am sure you've found."

I nodded. That was an understatement.

"This is a guide," she said. "A talisman. A holy relic to our family. It has been imbued with the magic of our blood. Not only did it bring you back in time and help you find me, but it is immensely valuable to both you and me."

It hit me hard, then. Harder than it had previously. This woman was my great-grandmother six or seven times back. My throat tightened. It wasn't quite like meeting my mother, but it was the closest I would come.

Grey gripped my hand, as if he could feel the turmoil inside me. I clung to him.

"I left it for you," she said. "Before my memory was taken by my father, I hid the book in the Shadow Guild tower, hoping that down the line, one of my children or their children would find it." She smiled. "It seems to have taken a while, if you are from the year 2020."

"It's helping you remember the memories that were taken," I said.

She nodded. "It is partially my magic, which is the same as yours. And partially the book itself, reminding me of what has led me here."

"Please tell me more. I want to understand what happened to you."

"I believe you know my father, Councilor Rasla, and what he has done," she said. I nodded, and she continued. "After using great magic to hide the Shadow Guild tower, he erased the memories of the townsfolk, including mine. No one can remember that there was a guild by that name. I remember feeling something lost inside my head. It became worse when he locked me inside my room, along with my baby." She rubbed her head. "It is all a bit of a mess in my memories. But my power allowed me to see glimpses of what he had done. I could read the story in the various things that I touched. Eventually, I understood enough of it."

"And you ran away."

"It was always a matter of time, whether or not I

discovered my father's terrible deed. He hated my child. Was glad when her father died of illness."

Anger shot through me.

She seemed to notice it and shook her head. "No. Don't be angry for me. I am moving forward, away from those terrible feelings and memories."

"That's why you're running from Guild City. To start over," I said.

She nodded. "My father is a monster. I can't live there anymore."

"What about the Shadow Guild? You don't want to fight to bring it back?" I asked. "It's your birthright." I pointed to the baby. "From what I understand, she is meant to lead it."

The woman smiled down at the baby. "Power for power's sake is a trap. Being born into a role you are forced to fill is a terrible fate." Her words rang with experience, and I couldn't help but think back to my fear of taking over the Shadow Guild as leader. It wasn't the same, though, was it?

"I want my child to be able to choose. It is wonderful to live among one's own kind, but Guild City has been tainted by my father. It is not a place she can live freely. Better to hide her magic in this world than to be forced to live a life of fear in that place."

"Are you speaking for yourself as well as for her?" I asked.

She smiled. "Perhaps I am."

"So you'll live as humans."

She nodded. "Perhaps. I will see where the road takes me."

"But what about the others in the Shadow Guild?" I asked. "Their place has been taken from them. Many were forced to leave Guild City. Those who stayed were made to feel like outcasts."

I *knew* I shouldn't be trying to change the past, but I couldn't help asking. It was all so terrible.

Her eyes darkened with sadness. "And that breaks my heart, but what is done is done. You are proof of that. Time has continued on, the Shadow Guild staying hidden until you found it. If you and I were to return to Guild City and change things, then the entire course of the future would be modified. People who need to be born might not be born, while others would die. I discovered my father's subterfuge too late, and too much time has passed." She reached out for me but drew her hand back before making contact. "And seeing you proves that I've made the right choice."

"Because I found the Shadow Guild?"

"And proved that the future has unfurled in the way I hoped it would. My line has continued. I have faith in fate and my path." She jostled the baby a bit. "I assume the future is a better place?"

I thought of it for a moment. "There is no one like your father in Guild City, so yes, I suppose. It's not a perfect place, and a lot of the world is a mess. But the

Shadow Guild is continuing. It *will* continue, once we clean it up a bit."

"And you are the leader?"

"That's what my friends tell me." Though I hadn't embraced it yet, that was for certain. Guilt struck me.

It was my heritage. And I was ignoring it.

"What of your family?" she asked. "How are they?"

"My father was a bastard, and I never knew my mother. But she must have had magic."

"Never knew her?"

"She died shortly after I was born."

"Tragic." She frowned. "Had she known she had magic, I imagine she would have left you a letter. Something to explain."

Maybe. I hoped so. "She may never have known. We lived in the human world."

"Oh, my." She shook her head. "What a path I have set us on, to live in the human world so long."

If my mother had survived, would we have found out what we were together?

I gripped Grey's hand hard, drawing support from him. He rubbed my back with his other hand, and I looked at the woman. "I need to know what I am. I only know what I can do, and even that is ever changing."

"You are coming into your power. It takes a while, with magic as strong as ours."

"I need it to be strong." I gestured to Grey. "We're Cursed Mates, and our time is running short. A seer has told me that I can save us and that the answer is in my past, but I have no idea how."

She frowned, her brow furrowing. "Really?"

"Yes. What are we? How do I break the curse?"

She bit her lip, clearly distressed. Her gaze moved between the two of us. "I did not anticipate this."

"Neither did I," Grey said. "But I want to spend my life with Carrow. Without your help, though, it's going to be a very short life."

The baby began to whimper, as if sensing its mother's distress, and she rocked it carefully, her eyes shadowed. Finally, she looked at me. "I don't know how our magic can possibly break the curse. But I can tell you what we are, at the very least."

I nodded, wanting her to spill it all quickly.

"You are a Soulceress, a member of the only known line in Britain. Maybe the world."

"Soulceress?" It was a mouthful.

She nodded. "We derive our power from our souls. From the souls of others, as well. It's why you can touch people and know things about them. You are reading their soul."

"And when I touch objects?"

"That power comes from your own soul."

I looked back at Grey. "Have you heard of these types of supernaturals?"

"Only by name," he said. "I never knew the extent of their power."

"But I can do more than read objects and people," I said. "I brought my friend back from the dead."

She smiled, tears sparking in her eyes. "That is a power so rare that only the strongest of us possess it. My grandmother did."

"How did I do it?"

"May I touch you so that I can understand the circumstances fully?" She lifted her ungloved hand. "I know the theory behind your magic, but understanding your situation will help.

I nodded and held out my hand, palm up. She gripped it gently, her hand cold and firm. But warmth flowed through me, her magic touching mine.

Was this what my power felt like to others?

It was nice.

Evangeline drew in a steady breath, and I could feel her magic inside me, poking around for answers. Finally, she opened her eyes and met my gaze, though she did not drop my hand.

"When you truly love someone—deeply and forever—your soul touches theirs. Bonds to it in an unbreakable way. If they die before you, and you have trouble letting them go, then their soul will resist death."

Shock raced through me. "I kept Beatrix on Earth? Like a ghost?"

"Not quite like a ghost. Ghosts are here of their own volition. They need magical energy to stay on this plane instead of being dragged to the afterlife, but they produce it on their own."

"Beatrix said that after she died, she was drawn to my friend Eve, a Fae."

Evangeline nodded. "This makes sense. When she died, your soul expended a massive amount of energy to draw her back from death. I believe she became a raven because it is tied to her magic and was an easier form to maintain. But she needed to find an energy source if she was to survive on Earth until you could find her again."

"So she found Eve."

"Yes. There is something about Eve's magic that gave Beatrix the power to stay on this plane. You were drawn to each other. No doubt she found Eve because fate wanted to help her find you. Once you had the book, it gave you the strength and focus to finish the spell that would keep her from death."

My mind was spinning. "So Beatrix is back for good and will live a normal life?"

"Yes. You have prevented her death this one time. But there's no guarantee you can do it again if another of your friends dies. Circumstances must be right. Once you yank them from the brink of death, their soul needs an energy source to sustain them until you can find them and bring them back for good."

I drew in a bracing breath. This was all so damned much. I looked at Grey, not liking where this was possibly leading us. "How does this help me break the curse on Grey and me?"

"That, I do not know. But I can feel that you aren't fully embracing your power."

"How can I embrace it if I don't know what it is?"

"We never know what the future holds for us, nor what we are truly capable of. Not until we are tested."

"And I haven't been tested yet?"

"Perhaps not." She shrugged. "But I do know that you have shied from your duty as leader of the Shadow Guild, and that cannot help."

"I thought you said you were running away so your children wouldn't be forced to serve as leader."

"*Forced* being the key word. But you are not forced, are you? You want it, I believe."

Icy fear stabbed me at the thought of so much responsibility. "I've just discovered I'm magical, now I'm meant to be a guild leader? It's crazy."

"Only if you let your fear drive you and stop you from growing. Stop you from taking your rightful place."

"And if I do this, my magic could grow in a way that helps me save Grey?"

"I believe it's possible, yes. You must embrace every-thing that you are and have faith in yourself if you want to be powerful enough to save him. To save yourself."

I heaved out a breath, worried.

She pressed the book into my hands. "Take this.

Claim your place and believe in yourself. That is your only way forward."

I gripped the book, hating that the solution to our problems was so vague and difficult. Believing in myself was a hell of a lot harder than accomplishing a set task, like fighting demons or finding a magical potion.

"That book will help you with your magic." Evangeline nodded to it. "Keep it safe, always, and use its power when you need it."

"Thank you."

She nodded and stood. My heart raced, my skin chilling. Our time was almost over. She was finished, it was obvious, and ready to make a run for it. Ready to put the wheel of my past in motion.

I stood. "Can I visit you?"

Her eyes flickered with surprise. "You mean use the book to return to this time and find me?"

I nodded. "Yes. You're the only living family I have."

"Living?" She smiled. "I suppose that depends on what timeline you are in."

I winced. She was right. She'd be dead and dust by the time I went back through the library.

"Perhaps you can visit," she said. "Go home and sort out this problem with your beau. Once you've embraced your magic fully, you'll know if you're strong enough to come back here. But it's a risk every time, remember. You must not change the past."

I sighed, my heart hurting. I couldn't come back. Not with so much at risk.

Grey stepped around to my side and met Evangeline's gaze. "Do you have enough money to start your new life?"

"Enough?" She nodded, though it was uncertain. "I have enough."

He frowned, then reached into his pocket and handed her a pouch like the one he'd given Mrs. Birch-Cleve. "Take this to help."

She took it and looked down at it, shaking her head. "How strange this day has been."

"No kidding." I hugged her briefly, trying not to squash the baby, then pulled back. "We'd best be going."

She nodded. "Good luck."

I gave her one last look, then turned. We hurried out of the garden, cutting our way through the crowd. There was so much to think about and talk about—like *what the hell was I supposed to do?*

But first, we needed to find Rasla and erase his memory of Grey so that his past wouldn't be modified.

We made it to the Haunted Hound in record time, passing through to Guild City a few moments later. It was late in the evening, the streetlamps illuminating the ancient city. People milled about, laughing and happy.

"Shall we go to his house?" I asked.

"Yes. That's the best place to start." He led the way, cutting through the city.

Coincidentally, the library was on the route to Rasla's house. I almost wished we could just dart in and head home, but it was well worth stopping and erasing Rasla's memory. There was no telling what kind of hell he'd cause for the other version of Grey.

We were only about twenty meters past the library when a shout sounded. "Devil!" Rasla's voice echoed down the empty street.

I stopped dead in my tracks, right alongside Grey. We stood in the middle of the road. It was entirely empty. Finding Rasla here was just the most incredible kind of luck. Whether good or bad, I wasn't sure.

I turned, spotting Rasla sprinting toward us. Two men followed him, both wearing the distinctive cloaks of sorcerers.

"I knew you were after my daughter," Rasla hissed at me. "Did you find her? You look like her, you know. I can't let you leave here."

"You're a stupid bastard," I said. No way I was telling him a thing about his daughter.

"You will stop at once," Grey said, his voice ringing with power.

Rasla laughed, pointing to his jacket. A gleaming red gem was pinned to the breast. "This protects me from your miserable power."

Shit. He must have been wearing it when Grey had tried to modify his mind before. That's how he'd resisted Grey's power.

Both of the sorcerers were wearing the charms as well. We'd need to do this the old-fashioned way, all without killing Rasla or his men.

Both sorcerers raised their hands, green light glowing around their palms.

Fear struck me, sharp and cold.

I'd seen this magic before. Grey had been hit by it at the Sorcerers' Guild, nearly dying. And he'd been stronger then.

The sorcerers hurled their deadly blasts of magic at us. The acid-green clouds shot through the air. I dove right, and Grey dove left. I slammed to the ground, skidding across the cobblestones.

Aching, I scrambled upright, still intact. The blast had missed me, though just barely. Frantically, I searched for Grey. He was already on his feet, sprinting toward one of the sorcerers. The bastard was recharging his power, his palm glowing faintly green.

I plunged my hand into my potion bag and withdrew a potion bomb. I had no idea what it did—there was no time to look. I just threw it, hurling it at the other sorcerer. He ducked.

His hand glowed green, and I didn't have long before he'd throw another blast at me. I sprinted for him, plunging my hand back into the satchel.

To my left, Grey reached the sorcerer before he could hurl his magic. He drew back his fist and punched him so hard in the face that the sorcerer wheeled backward, landing hard on the ground.

He lay still, unconscious.

Grey turned toward Rasla, who stood only ten feet away. He stalked toward him.

I pulled out another potion bomb and hurled it at the sorcerer who had almost charged up his second blast. It slammed into his shoulder. He gasped, going to his knees. I charged him, my eyes on the glowing green orb in his hand. It was nearly at full power. He'd hurl it at me any second.

I braced myself, ready to dodge the blast if he threw it before I reached him.

He drew back his arm, then threw.

Only, instead of hurling it at me, he chucked it at Grey, who held Rasla by the lapels, speaking harshly into his face.

"Grey!" I screamed, reaching for him.

The green magic slammed into his back.

17

———

GREY

The explosive force of the blast seemed to pulverize my insides. Pain like I'd never felt. An atom bomb inside my chest. My vision blacked, and my breathing stopped.

Dying.

There was no other end to this.

I dropped to my knees in a total state of shock. There was silence all around—deadly, deafening silence that had to be false. It was only this silent when you lost your hearing.

Or when you were dead.

A scream broke through the quiet, piercing my mind, dragging me back to the present. Agony still suffused every inch of me, but I managed to force my eyes open. Through bleary vision, I spotted a confused Rasla staring at me.

The charm that had been pinned to his lapel was gone, and he blinked in a slow, befuddled manner.

I'd torn off the protective charm and erased his memory right before I'd been hit. What about the sorcerers? I didn't need them making hell for my former self. It was almost impossible to keep my thoughts in order, but I forced every ounce of energy that I had toward the task.

I might be dying now—I was *definitely* dying now—but if I didn't clean up this mess for my past self, then history might change and keep me from ever meeting Carrow.

I couldn't lose the time I'd had with her.

The thought gave me strength.

She appeared at my side a half moment later, dropping to her knees. "Grey!"

She touched me gently, her hands running over my body, searching for wounds. I leaned into her touch, drawing strength from her. She wouldn't find any wounds on the outside, but I already knew that I was running on the fumes of death.

Still on my knees, I reached up and grabbed Rasla's coat, pulling him down to face me. I used all the magic I had left to say, "Forget this ever happened or that you have any quarrel with me. If your men speak of it, they are lying."

He nodded, his gaze unfocused and his mouth slack. "Go."

He turned and walked off, moving slowly.

"Grey." Carrow moved around to face me, shoving a tiny vial into my hands. "Here. The last healing potion. Take it."

The cork had already been removed, so I tossed it back.

The liquid ran down my throat and filled my belly, but I only felt a fraction of its power. The pain still surged, and nausea followed in its wake.

The curse had its hooks fully into me.

It had been trying to drag me away from this world for so long, growing stronger every time I was injured. This would be the last straw. I could feel the ether tugging on me even now, the curse determined to pull me away from Carrow and the life that I had almost had.

A life of light and love.

"Are you all right?" she demanded, her voice wavering. "Is the potion working?"

"I'm fine." I had minutes left, maybe. We needed to get out of here. If I didn't survive, I couldn't leave Carrow here with my body. *Would* my body stay behind when I left?

I had no idea. Couldn't risk it. Too much to ask of her.

"Help me up, if you can." The words tasted sour as they left my lips.

Tears rolled down her face as she pulled me to my feet. Every part of me felt broken, shattered beyond repair. The sorcerer's magic had rent me inside, the blast doing irreparable damage.

Once, I might have survived it. Now, not a chance.

Carrow tucked herself under my arm to help support me, and I leaned on her, hating it. She shouldn't have to do this. Shouldn't have to be here for this.

I could only imagine what I would be feeling if I thought she were about to die. Utter devastation. The idea that she might hold that depth of feeling for me seemed almost laughable. But from the tears that streamed down her face, it also seemed almost possible.

My heart thundered.

Her scent wrapped around me as we walked, rousing the beast inside me. It wanted her blood, wanted me to drink to save us both.

This was my last chance. If I took her blood now, I would survive this. She would not, but her blood would not only break the curse, it would undo the damage of the sorcerer's magic. It would make me whole again.

I forced the beast back, unwilling to even consider it.

"We're almost there," she said. "The library is right up here, and we'll be home in no time. We'll fix you right up with more healing potions."

The sea could be made of healing potions, and it wouldn't be enough. I said nothing.

We staggered toward the library, finding it locked at

this late hour. Carrow leaned back and kicked open the door, hitting it so hard that the wood around the lock splintered and it swung open.

"I guess fear gives extra strength," she said as she helped pull me inside.

The cavernous library was dark save for a few fairy lights floating near the ceiling. Our footsteps echoed as we staggered toward the back of the library. My strength was waning, and I could feel myself putting more weight on Carrow.

She plowed onward, dragging me behind her.

"We've got this," she said, her voice trembling. "You're going to be okay."

"Of course." The words almost took the last of my breath.

Finally, we reached the very back of the library. The empty aisle called to me, the glowing light a beacon of hope. Not that I'd survive this, but that we'd at least make it back to our time for Carrow.

She pulled the small book out of her pocket, and we entered the aisle. The magic pulsed around us, bright and warm. My heartbeat began to slow as we entered deeper into the aisle, my vision starting to go dark at the edges.

Not yet.

I wanted one last look at her face.

I fought the pull of the afterlife, grateful when I felt the ether tugging on me. It caught us both and spun us through time. I gripped Carrow hard, determined not to lose her here.

A moment later, solid ground appeared beneath my feet. I staggered, the ground calling to me. Carrow tried to keep me up, her grip strong. We managed to get out of the stacks and into the cavernous space of the main library, but I was too heavy. I staggered to my knees, going down hard.

"Grey!" She followed me down, trying to slow my fall.

I hit the floor anyway, the tile cold beneath my feverish skin.

"Grey, you must drink from me." Her voice broke as she held her wrist to my mouth. "You need strength. The blow was too much."

I turned my mouth away, nearly insensible as the afterworld called to me. The beast within me roared, trying to force me to follow her commands. There was still time. Time to save us both. The beast and me.

Not Carrow.

I would *never*.

I looked up at her, wanting her face to be the last thing I saw. My voice rasped as I said, "I love you."

Why hadn't I said the words before? Why hadn't I shown her more?

What wasted time.

"Please, Grey. Don't go." Tears sounded in her voice. Rolled down her face. "I love you. I love you."

The words cloaked me in warmth as the darkness crept in. Nearly blind, I stole one last look at her. She was the sun, glowing golden above me, a promise of all that could have been and all that I didn't deserve.

We'd almost done it.

Almost.

Carrow

Grey went limp on the floor. His energy disappeared from the air, and I was alone.

Alone.

Something inside me broke, shattering into a thousand pieces. My scream echoed in the cavernous space. Frantically, I pulled at his shoulders, trying to drag him back. To make him stand, healthy and whole. "I love you. I love you."

I couldn't stop repeating the words, couldn't get ahold of myself. Everything was frantic inside me, everything terrible. I was pure energy, pure emotion.

On the ground, his body began to disappear.

I clutched at him, trying to keep him with me. Was this normal? Why was this happening? His form faded even more, becoming nearly transparent.

"Grey, don't go. Grey!"

Seconds later, he was entirely gone. I sat alone in the dark library, the air so still that it almost suffocated me. My mind went blank with pain and loss.

"Carrow!" Seraphia's voice sounded from the other side of the library, concern in her tone. She hurried toward me and fell to her knees at my side. "Carrow? Where's Grey? What's happened?"

I looked up at her, vision blurry with tears. "Gone. Gone."

"Where?"

"The curse took him. We were too late." I pressed a hand to the cold stone tile beneath me. "He was right here."

Seraphia looked down, as if she might see him. "It just happened?"

I sucked in a ragged breath, my throat so tight I almost couldn't manage to get the air in. "He was hit by a sorcerer's magic. It was too much. The damage was too much. He's been weakening, the afterworld pulling harder. And it was just too much."

I wanted to scream again, but Seraphia gripped my shoulders, shaking me hard as she commanded, "Breathe. In and out."

I did as she ordered, my shaking beginning to subside.

"Keep going," she said. "Get some oxygen into your brain so you can think."

I nodded blindly, scrubbing away my tears as I

sucked air into my lungs. As she'd promised, my mind began to clear. Thoughts returned in a more rational way, driving out the desperate fear and loss.

This wasn't over.

I wouldn't let it be over.

I'd brought back Beatrix. I would bring him back as well.

This was what fate had been maneuvering for all along. It was clear now.

I surged to my feet. "Where's Eve?"

"Asleep, I suppose." Seraphia rose, a frown on her face. "Why?"

"Grey. I need to find Grey." I lifted the skirt of my heavy dress, barely feeling its weight, and sprinted toward the door.

Seraphia followed, but I didn't wait for her to catch up. I raced out into the street and turned right, heading toward Eve's. The night was quiet as I ran, the moon high overhead. Grey had to be there. He had to be with her.

Her building was dark as I approached, every window black.

"Eve!" I screamed, pounding on the door. "Eve!"

"I'm calling her," Seraphia's voice sounded from my side. "She's on the top floor. Might not hear you.'

I looked down at her and saw her bare feet and legs. She wore sleep shorts and a ratty old T-shirt. No shoes.

She'd run all the way through the city barefoot behind me.

My throat tightened again.

The phone in her hands rang, and I kept banging on the door. I was two seconds away from breaking it down.

Eve answered Seraphia's call on the third ring, her voice annoyed. "What's going on? It's late as hell."

I grabbed the phone. "I'm at your flat. Let us in."

"I'm at the shop."

Shit.

It wasn't far. I shoved the phone back at Seraphia and sprinted down the street, headed the short distance to her shop. The lights glowed golden from inside, beckoning me with hope.

He would be there. Just like Beatrix, he would be there.

I shoved my way into the shop, finding Eve in her back room, potion ingredients spilled all over the tables. She looked up at me, eyes tired and questioning. "What's going on?"

"Where is he?" I demanded. "Grey?"

"What?" Eve frowned.

"He's gone. Dead." The words tumbled over themselves. "Like Beatrix was. But my magic could keep him from death. He'd need a power source like Beatrix did, though. He'd need you."

Confusion flashed across her face, and I realized that my partial sentences probably sounded crazy. She hadn't heard the whole story from Evangeline like I just had. She didn't understand.

I drew in a deep breath to calm myself. It didn't really work, but at least I wasn't screaming anymore. I searched the room around her, trying to get a feel for Grey. Was he here?

Would he turn into a bird?

I had no idea.

That had been part of Beatrix's magic. Maybe a bat? He was a vampire, after all. Or were vampire bats just something out of old cartoons? It seemed too ridiculous. No way he was a bat.

"What's going on, Carrow?" Eve's voice was calm and clear, and I clung to it, trying to join her in the realm of the rational.

"In the last thirty minutes, have you felt another life force appear around you?" I asked. "An animal or something?"

She shook her head. "There's been nothing."

"Did you feel Beatrix when she arrived?"

"Um..." She frowned. "Not particularly, to be honest."

I nodded. Okay. Okay. That meant he could still be there then. But *where?*

I spun in a circle, searching. Eve looked questioningly at Seraphia, who shrugged. I ignored them, trying to gather my thoughts. I had the power to bring him back. Not only had Evangeline told me so, but I could feel it. I just needed to figure out how.

There was more to this than I realized. I staggered to the shelf and sank to the ground, the floor hard against my butt. Blindly, I stared into space, trying to piece it all together.

This was a puzzle, and there was a missing piece.

I just needed to find it.

A half second later, Cordelia charged into the room, Mac at her heels. Beatrix trailed in last.

"What's going on?" Mac demanded. "Cordelia freaked out, but I can't understand her. What's wrong?"

Cordelia sprinted to a stop next to me, tugging at my dress sleeve with her little paws. *What's wrong? I felt it. It's terrible. What's wrong?*

"Grey," I whispered.

"Oh, shit." Mac leaned back against the bookshelves, clearly understanding right away.

"What?" Beatrix demanded.

"Tell us what you're thinking," Eve said. "Work it out with us."

Cordelia climbed on my lap, heavy and warm. I blinked, looking at all of my friends. The words spilled from my mouth, the whole story. Eve was right. If there was a clue in there somewhere, they could help find it.

I told them all about the past, and Rasla and Evangeline, and my history with the Shadow Guild. They listened quietly, asking the occasional question.

When I finally finished, Mac frowned. "It's obvious, isn't it?"

"Is it?" I sank my fingers into Cordelia's rough fur.

"Evangeline was clear that you haven't embraced your role in the Shadow Guild yet. Or your magic. You haven't believed in yourself. It's exactly what I told you earlier."

I nodded, sucking in a breath. She was right. That was the one big thing Evangeline had told me to do, and I hadn't done it yet. Maybe that was the problem.

"I've got to get up," I said to Cordelia. She scrambled off, and I stood. "Let's go to the Shadow Guild."

It called to me now, in the way that Grey had called to me. Maybe he was there. Or maybe he really was with Eve and I wasn't strong enough to sense him yet.

I was going to be.

If that meant visiting the Shadow Guild and finding a way to embrace my magic, then I was going to do it.

The five of us hurried down the street through the dark night. I could feel Beatrix's confusion—everyone's confusion, for that matter—but fortunately, none of them asked any questions. I didn't think I could answer, anyway, especially since I barely knew the answers myself.

We reached the courtyard in front of our tower a few moments later. Quinn stood there, confused. He was dressed in loose sleep pants and a T-shirt, his trainers partially unlaced. His auburn hair was messy around his head, and he looked confused.

"Why are we here?" he asked. "I woke up and felt like I had to come."

The Shadow Guild must have called to him. Because this was all of us now—our entire ragtag little guild.

Through my grief and terror, the slightest bit of warmth filled my chest.

"Long story," Mac said. "But we're here for Carrow."

He nodded and then turned, opening the door. We filed into the room, and I walked toward the big chair near the cold, quiet hearth.

Somehow, the sight of it made my skin chill even more. Either fear or doubt, I didn't know. It was the same thing I'd felt before. But this time, I ignored it.

If that was the leader's chair, then hell, I was going to sit in it.

I sucked in a deep breath and didn't so much as pause, just spun around and plopped my butt into it.

Nothing happened. I gripped the arms and looked at my friends.

I wanted to ask them if I should really be there.

Me?

Me, with the wonky magic and history of being raised in the human world?

And yet, my history was more than that. It was generations of Soulceresses, leaders of the Shadow Guild.

I closed my eyes, drew in a deep breath, and called on my magic. I let it fill me, glowing warm within. Trembling, I gripped the arms of the chair. The wood was smooth beneath my fingertips.

I wanted to know more. Wanted to understand this role and my place in it. How I could embrace it more fully.

I used my power, trying to draw information from the wood beneath my fingertips. Generations of my ancestors had sat here. It might have taken me a long time to find my way home, but I *had*.

Finally, I was here.

The air warmed around me, vibrating with energy. I pulled out the book that Evangeline had given me, gripping it tight. I didn't need to be able to read the strange symbols inside to feel their power and their history. It sang through me.

My magic turned inward, filling my soul and seeming to pull my consciousness away from the present. One moment, there was nothing behind my eyelids. The next, I stood at the entrance to a tunnel.

It stretched out in front of me, dark and cold. Beckoning. Fear sliced through me.

Could I do it?

Walk through that tunnel and find what was on the other side?

I had to.

Somehow, I knew that I had to. Answers were on the other side. Or maybe strength. Growth. Something.

I took one slow step forward, then another. Everything inside me screamed with anxiety, but I kept going, walking into the darkness. The future was unknown and so was my role in it, but if I just kept moving forward and *trying,* then I would get somewhere.

The air grew colder as I walked deeper into the tunnel but, somehow, I felt less alone. The future beckoned to me, and I knew the tunnel would end.

Almost abruptly, it did. I exited into a glowing white room, feeling my body return to the leader's chair in the Shadow Guild tower.

All around me, figures appeared. Men and women, most of them dressed in ancient garb. I spotted Evangeline, standing next to a woman who looked just like her. Her daughter, maybe. The baby I'd seen, all grown up.

A feeling of warmth and love surrounded me. This was my family. The long line of them—gone, but not entirely.

A woman stepped out from the crowd, immediately recognizable, even though I'd never seen so much as a photo of her.

My mother.

I surged upright, moving toward her. She held open her arms, hugging me tightly. Joy exploded inside me, warmth and strength.

"You are strong," she whispered against my ear. "You can do anything."

"I love you."

She hugged me tighter. "I love you, too. More than anything. I'm always with you, even if you don't see me."

My soul seemed to expand, filling with the love and support of the family I'd never met. I wanted to stay like this forever, hugging my mother in the perfect silence of this magical space.

But Grey.

I couldn't stay.

He needed me.

The Shadow Guild needed me.

As if she understood, my mother drew back. She looked at me with such love and pride that I thought I might explode on the spot.

"You can do this." She squeezed my arms tightly, then disappeared.

The rest followed, leaving me in the real Shadow Guild. My friends stared at me, eyes wide and concerned.

My family.

I had more than just my blood family. I had *them*. My chosen family.

18

———

CARROW

Suddenly, everything felt so much better.

"Carrow? Are you all right?" Mac asked.

"Fine."

"You look a bit pale." Beatrix frowned. "And you zoned out there for a while. Very weird."

I stood, my soul full and my magic strong. Everything was calmer in my mind, though fear still nipped at my heels. I shoved it back.

"You look good there." Mac gestured to the chair. "Real natural."

"Feels okay, too." I smiled, though it wasn't a large one. My heart thundered as my mind raced. "I need to find Grey."

"I don't think he's with me," Eve said. "Not the way Beatrix was. I haven't seen anything out of the ordinary."

I clutched the book, my mind racing. Where would Grey go for strength? For the energy required to stay on this plane?

Suddenly, it occurred to me.

"I need to go." I stood, shoving the book into the pocket of my full skirts.

"Care to clarify?" Mac asked.

"I think I know where Grey is."

"Want company?" Seraphia asked.

"Part way there?" I looked at them all. "To his tower?"

"Sure," Quinn said.

The rest nodded. I hurried from the building, unable to keep myself from running. I sprinted through the quiet streets of Guild City, scaring pigeons and annoying night-hunting cats when I disturbed their prey. My friends kept up with me as we raced along.

Not a single one of them had any idea what was going on, but they stuck with me. It gave me strength, the same way that seeing my mother and other members of my family had.

Finally, I reached the courtyard in front of Grey's tower. The building rose tall and dark against the night sky, the glass a deep, blood red. The doormen stood by the entrance, their gazes impassive.

They still had no idea about Grey.

I wouldn't tell them.

Both bowed, then opened the door for us. I hurried into the lobby, spotting Miranda by the front podium. She wore a long black silk robe, her hair piled on her head. Her eyes were red, as if she'd been crying, and she stood still as a statue.

"You know," I said.

She nodded, gaze vacant. "I felt it."

"I need to go to his quarters."

Her gaze sharpened on me. "Why?"

"I'm going to try to bring him back."

Confusion flickered in her eyes, but she asked no questions. "You'll find it unlocks for you." She gestured to my friends. "They can wait in the bar."

I nodded. She was right. As much as I valued their support, they shouldn't be in Grey's private flat. I turned to them. "Thank you for coming."

"Duh," Mac said.

Everyone else's expressions reflected the same. Of course they had come. Miranda led them away, and I turned and raced down the hall. When I reached his door, my heart began to thunder, my skin chilling.

Please work.

I prayed I was right about this.

Quickly, I pressed my palm to the door. Magic sparked under my hand, and the locking charm broke. I pushed open the door, stepping into the quiet silence of the room.

It was so different than how I'd seen it last. Modern and clean-lined. The contrast reminded me that I was still in the heavy dress, but it didn't matter.

I strode to the bedroom, moving quickly toward the massive, enchanted window that revealed an expansive view of the Carpathian Mountains.

I'd admired this view since I'd first been in this room. Only recently had I learned what it meant to him.

Please be right.

I strode toward it, already anticipating the cold. When I reached it, I didn't hesitate. I just stepped toward the huge window, praying that I wouldn't smash my foot on glass that I didn't fully believe existed.

It went right through the glass as if there were nothing there at all. My foot sank into cold snow on the other side, and I stepped fully through the window.

Icy wind buffeted me, snow pricking against my skin. In front of me, mountains rose high against the sparkling night sky. A full moon and thousands of stars shone on the snow, making it look like the earth was frosted in crystals.

"Grey!" I screamed, my voice becoming lost in the wind. "Grey!"

There was silence. I staggered forward, sinking up to my shins in the powder. It slipped down the tops of my tall boots, chilling my skin. I barely noticed.

My heart began to pound as I searched for Grey. How would he appear? Was he even here?

No.

I couldn't doubt. I wouldn't.

He was here. I would find him.

He'd said this place gave him strength. That it spoke to something in his soul, rejuvenating him. *This* was his Eve.

I drew in a deep breath and called out again, tears pricking my eyes. I might be confident he was here, but I was terrified I wouldn't manage this. Not because I didn't believe in myself, but because I couldn't face a life without him. It wasn't a world I wanted to live in.

Snow fell all around, sticking to my hair and dress. The cold seeped into my veins, but I welcomed it. It made me feel alive. Present.

I fell to my knees in the snow, sucking in a huge lungful of cold air. Magic sparked through me as I took in the mountains ahead. Cold, hard, strong. But beneath them, far in the earth, was a core of heat.

Just like Grey.

Of course this place spoke to him.

This place *was* him.

I stared at the mountains through the snow and called on my magic, pulling the book from my skirts. Evangeline's face whispered though my mind as I clutched it tight. My mother's face. The faces of all of my family.

Power surged through me, strong and fierce. Just like

when I'd tried to bring back Beatrix. My soul filled with it, warming me from within.

The wind began to circle around me, the snow swirling in a cyclone. Energy crackled on the air, joining with my magic. It was so powerful that I felt like I was flying, my entire being lighting from within.

All around me, I could feel Grey. His strength, his honor, his kindness. He was with me. I sank my free hand into the cold snow, clutching a handful tight.

Power flowed between me and the night, between me and Grey. Determination replaced fear.

I could do this.

I would do this.

Suddenly, I could smell the firelight and whisky scent that was so distinctly Grey. Could hear the thunder of his magic, despite the fact that the night was clear.

The wind whipped faster and faster, so much magic contained within it. Energy exploded within me, my power going wild. Tears poured from my eyes, grief and hope and terror and joy.

The wind began to slow, the snow so thick that I could no longer see the mountains beyond. It coalesced in front of me, forming the shape of a man. Forming Grey.

One moment, there was only whiteness around me.

The next, there was Grey.

Healthy. Whole.

"Grey." I fell toward him through the snow.

He pulled me up, his hands strong and warm and *real.*

I threw my arms around him, hugging him tight. "You're okay. You're okay."

He clutched me close to him, his warmth surrounding me. His scent and strength filled me. "You brought me back."

"Of course. Of course." I pulled back and kissed him, my lips cold against his warmer ones. "I was so scared I'd lost you."

He kissed me again, seeming to try to absorb me into him. I hugged him close, never wanting to let him go. He was having none of it, though. He pulled back and looked at me, his eyelashes now studded with snow. I could only imagine what I looked like. A snowman, perhaps.

"Why the bloody hell are we in the freezing cold?" he asked.

"We're in Carpathia. In the mountains you love. I went through the portal in your flat."

Confusion wrinkled his brow. "Why the bloody hell would you do that?"

"This is the place that gives you strength. You said it yourself. Just like Eve's magic kept Beatrix going until I could find her again, this place kept you going."

He smiled, shaking his head. "You ninny. It wasn't mountains or snow or cold that kept me here. It was you. Since the moment I died, it was your light that kept me here."

"What?" Confusion flashed. "But I tried to bring you back before. It didn't work."

"You didn't believe in yourself yet. You hadn't fully embraced your magic. You needed to find yourself fully at the Shadow Guild for it to work. I could feel the difference in you once you had."

"Oh, my gosh." I looked around at the snow, at the freezing landscape that could have killed me. "So I imagined that this place did it?"

He nodded. "I believe so. I love these mountains, but they aren't you. They aren't what kept me going."

I threw my arms around him again, so blessedly grateful to have him back with me. He pulled me up into his arms, sweeping me out of the snow. I clung to him, my enormous skirts covered in snow. He strode through the drifts, exiting the freezing landscape and arriving back in his flat.

I leaned up and kissed him, determined never to let him go ever again.

19

___

Two days later, after we'd cleaned up the snowdrift in Grey's flat and confirmed that we hadn't changed any of the present while in the past, Grey and I returned to Silviu's Castle. I raced down the stone stairs into the depths, Grey at my side. We needed to see the seer— needed the confirmation that we'd broken the curse.

I was certain we had, and Grey no longer felt the beast inside him, but I needed to hear it.

We'd approached the castle under the cover of night like last time, but we'd come with a better plan. Meeting Silviu again was out of the question, so the Shadow Guild had come along. Mac, Eve, Seraphia, Quinn, Beatrix, and Cordelia were all currently outside, creating a massive disturbance on the side of Silviu's mountain.

We'd waited while they set off hundreds of Eve's fireworks. Unlike human fireworks, they formed monsters and armies, all made of light and fire. It looked like a legitimate attack. It would act like one as well, fooling Silviu for at least a little while. Long enough for us to get our answers, hopefully. And as expected, Silviu had run outside, along with Remington and all the guards in the castle.

Grey and I had made our move, darting through the main entrance and heading toward the seer's underground lair.

"This is how we should have entered the first time," he said as we raced down the stairs. "I never should have expected him to be reasonable."

"It worked out in the end." I panted, exhausted from the all the sprinting. "How far are we?"

"We're nearly there," he said. "Only a couple more flights."

"Thank God." There were so many that I'd lost track. If we ran into Silviu, we could fight him. With the Shadow Guild at our backs, we could take out the creepy vampire and all his guards. But it'd be better to avoid it.

Finally, we reached the bottom of the stairs. The enormous cavern echoed with our footsteps, the cool mist making goosebumps rise on my skin. Long icicles hung from the black rock walls.

"I can't believe it lives down here," I said.

"I'm not sure *live* is the right word for it." Grey reached for my hand, and I gripped his tightly.

As we walked deeper into the cavern, I prayed the seer would come to us. Prayed it would have the answers we sought.

The mist surrounded me, touching every inch of my skin with an inquisitiveness that shouldn't be possible. But this mist *was* the seer. It began to swirl, a breeze making my hair rise off my neck, then coalesced in front of us, thickening until it fell to the ground with a loud splash and formed a puddle. The opalescent water lapped at the tips of my boots.

It was all so eerily similar to last time, when we'd started out on this journey.

The water rose upward, forming the same ethereal figure with indistinct features and no discernable gender. Wisdom radiated from the seer, making me feel warm inside.

Grey and I bowed, rising slowly.

"You are back," the seer said, its voice slow and steady.

"We've broken the curse," I replied.

"We believe," Grey said. "But we would appreciate if you could confirm it for us."

The seer moved around us, circling us slowly. My

heart raced as it drifted, its magic wafting around us. When it returned to stand in front of us, its form slipped into Grey, the white mist disappearing.

He stiffened, his brow furrowing. I shivered, remembering the odd sensation from our last visit.

After a few minutes, it drifted back out of his body.

Well? I bit back the words.

"The curse is indeed broken," it said. "Your death severed that dark bond, though you are still mates."

Joy, warm and bright, filled my chest. "And when I brought him back, everything went okay?" I hoped I hadn't screwed something up for him.

"He is as he should be," the seer said. "No longer immortal. Still a vampire, but mortal now, like born vampires."

Grey's shoulders relaxed, and I knew it was with relief. He'd been worried about living forever, having to watch me die.

"Is there anything else you could possibly tell us?" I asked.

"Hmm." It watched us, crossing its arms. Clearly debating something. "Did you cause the commotion outside a short while ago?"

Grey hesitated, then said, "Yes, that is our doing."

It was impossible to be sure, but I thought it smiled. "Good. That Silviu is a miserable bastard. I enjoy his annoyance. Therefore, I will tell you that you will grow old and die together. When your time on Earth is up, you'll travel to the same afterlife." Its voice sharpened. "But don't use that as an excuse to go do stupid, dangerous things."

Elation exploded inside me. It was more than I could ever hope for. More than I could dream.

"Thank you," I said. "Thank you so much."

Grey inclined his head. "You have my sincerest gratitude."

The seer nodded. "As I should. Now I suggest that you leave here before Silviu's guards return."

We thanked the seer again, then ran from the cavern. As I raced up the stairs, my heart felt like it was going to explode from the joy of it.

We'd done it. Broken the curse. Saved our own lives. And we had a future together. An amazing, beautiful future.

A few moments later, we raced out the front door and away from the fireworks on the west side of the mountain. Silviu and his men appeared to be figuring out that it was all a trick. In the distance, behind a rock outcropping, I spotted my friends. Cordelia sat on Quinn's broad shoulder, and the others gathered round, peeping their heads up from behind the rocks.

They waved, gesturing us closer. We sprinted toward them.

"Well?" Mac demanded as we neared.

"We're good!" I said, grinning wildly. "It worked!"

"Then let's get the hell out of here." Eve scowled up

at the scene in the distance. "They're going to start looking for the cause of that little show soon."

I nodded, beaming at them all. My eyes met Beatrix's, and she smiled widely. "This is crazy," she said.

"Isn't it?" It made me so damned happy to see her here. To see them all here. "Come on. Let's go."

The seven of us raced down the mountain, with me leading the way.

EPILOGUE

GREY

The coast of Cornwall was bloody lovely on a sunny afternoon. Sunlight sparkled off deep blue waves, and wildflowers dotted the green grass that topped the cliffs.

Beside me, Carrow looked impossibly beautiful, her golden hair gleaming like the sun. She *was* the sun.

"I think we've almost found it." She pulled me along the coast path. "I can feel it."

We were searching for Evangeline's grave. Her friends were having a picnic a couple of miles down the coast, and we would join them once we were done.

But this was a journey just for us.

And Cordelia, who ran far ahead of us on the path.

A week ago, after we'd visited the seer in Silviu's castle, we'd begun to look for the grave. Carrow wanted to do it, and I wanted her to be happy.

She'd saved me. She's saved *us*.

"I think this is it." Carrow pointed up the hill to a spot about twenty yards off the path. "See the pile of stones?"

"I do. Let's go visit." I held a bunch of flowers we'd gathered along the coast.

Without Evangeline, we wouldn't have each other.

Carrow laughed as we ran through the grass, headed up the hill toward the grave. For the briefest moment, I had a vision of what we must look like. It was an out-of-body experience.

I was running through grass. Laughing.

It was so far away from the interminable years of my immortality that it seemed like a different planet. This one was in color, fully and brightly. The air smelled better, the grass felt softer, and everything tasted divine.

Carrow was here.

We slowed to a stop in front of the pile of stones. They were arranged in a neat pyramid, and pink flowers grew between them, trembling on the cool sea breeze.

"It really is her." Carrow knelt. "I can feel it."

I joined her, laying the flowers on the cairn. "She's with you always."

Carrow nodded, her eyes gleaming slightly. "She and

my mother and all the rest of my family." She turned to me and kissed me. "And you, too."

"Always."

THANK YOU FOR READING!

I hope you enjoyed reading this book as much as I enjoyed writing it. Reviews are *so* helpful to authors. I really appreciate all reviews, both positive and negative. If you want to leave one, you can do so at Amazon or GoodReads.

ACKNOWLEDGMENTS

Thank you, Ben, for everything. There would be no books without you.

Thank you to Jena O'Connor, Lexi George, and Ash Fitzsimmons for your excellent editing. The book is immensely better because of you!

Thank you to Orina Kafe for the beautiful cover art.

Thank you so much for reading *Carrow's Series*! As you know by now (if you generally read the Author's Note), this is where I like to mention the historical elements in the book—both interesting tidbits and where I might have deviated from history. There weren't a large number of new historical elements in *Cursed Mate*, but one of the most distinct was Silviu's castle in Transylvania.

In preparation for this book, I made a trip to Romania to see Vlad the Impaler's birthplace and the castle that is associated with him. I knew that it wouldn't look like the Transylvania of American movies (largely populated by dark, creepy castles and rainy old villages) but I was surprised by the extreme difference between what our movies depicted and the truth.

Quite simply, Transylvanian villages are the loveliest, cheeriest villages I'd ever seen. They give the Cotswolds a run for their money, albeit with a different style of architecture. But when it comes to writing a vampire book, one can't write "he returned to the land of his birth, which looked like the Romanian version of a Norman Rockwell painting." So I leaned into the creepy Dracula castle vibe, but it was fun to think of the contrast while doing so. If you're interested in getting a look at what I'm talking about, do a Google image search fro **Sighișoara**, the birthplace of Vlad the Impaler.

Another historical element in the story was the Mages' Coffeehouse. It first appeared in *Dark Secrets*, where I discuss the history of English coffeehouses more fully. But I thought I should mention that the Mages Coffeehouse, which appeared in Guild City in 1642 in this book, predates the first English Coffeehouse by 10 years (that was a coffeehouse established in Oxford in 1652 by a Jewish entrepreneur). So, depending on how you look at it, the Mages Coffeehouse is either inaccurate in its timing for appearing in England, or it was the first :-) I should also note that it would be unusual for a coffee house to allow women at that time (thank you to my editor Lauren Simpson for pointing that out to me!). Guild City is far advanced in terms of gender equality compared to the human world.

The garden at Councilor Rasla's house was based on the Elizabethan Garden in Plymouth England, and the house took its inspiration from the Elizabethan House museum that is associated with the garden.

Lastly, in this book, Carrow is revealed to be a Soulceress. If you've read my paranormal romance series, you might recognize Soulceress as the title of the second book. I came up with Carrow's magical talents before I figured out *what* she was, exactly, so when it came time to name Carrow's species, I kept returning to the word Soulceress. I liked it so much that I decided I would use it again and it could be a different look a similar concept. So if you aren't interested in a totally different take on Soulceresses, consider reading *Soulceress*. It is set in a different magical world (this one populated by immortals) but it has many similar themes to the Shadow guild world.

Thank you again for going on Carrow and Grey's adventure with them. This isn't the last we'll see of the Guild City crew. Seraphia will be returning in Autumn 2020, and her name isn't really Seraphia. Be sure to check it out to find out why she's been such a mess lately!

ABOUT LINSEY

Before becoming a writer, Linsey Hall was a nautical archaeologist who studied shipwrecks from Hawaii and the Yukon to the UK and the Mediterranean. She credits fantasy and historical romances with her love of history and her career as an archaeologist. After a decade of tromping around the globe in search of old bits of stuff that people left lying about, she settled down and started penning her own romance novels. Her Dragon's Gift series draws upon her love of history and the paranormal elements that she can't help but include.